The BALLAD Of
PECKHAM RYE

The BALLAD Of
PECKHAM RYE

MURIEL
SPARK

AVON BOOKS  NEW YORK

AVON BOOKS
A division of
The Hearst Corporation
105 Madison Avenue
New York, New York 10016

Copyright © 1960 by Muriel Spark
Front cover painting copyright © 1990 by Brad Holland
Inside cover author photograph by Mark Alan Gompertz
Published by arrangement with Georges Borchardt, Inc.
Library of Congress Catalog Card Number: 90-93172
ISBN: 0-380-70936-8

First Avon Books Trade Printing: November 1990

Printed in the U.S.A.

OPM 10 9 8 7 6 5 4 3 2 1

For
ROBIN
with love

⫷ 1 ⫸

"Get away from here, you dirty swine," she said.

"There's a dirty swine in every man," he said.

"Showing your face round here again," she said.

"Now, Mavis, now, Mavis," he said.

She was seen to slam the door in his face, and he to press the bell, and she to open the door again.

"I want a word with Dixie," he said. "Now, Mavis, be reasonable."

"My daughter," Mavis said, "is not in." She slammed the door in his face.

All the same, he appeared to consider the encounter so far satisfactory. He got back into the little Fiat and drove away along the Grove and up to the Common where he parked outside the Rye Hotel. Here he lit a cigarette, got out, and entered the saloon bar.

Three men of retired age at the far end turned from the television and regarded him. One of them nudged his friend. A woman put her hand to her chin and turned to her companion with a look.

His name was Humphrey Place. He was that fellow that walked out on his wedding a few weeks ago. He walked across to the "White Horse" and drank one bitter. Next he visited the "Morning Star" and the "Heaton Arms." He finished up at the "Harbinger."

The pub door opened and Trevor Lomas walked in. Trevor was seen to approach Humphrey and hit him on the mouth. The barmaid said, "Outside, both of you."

"It wouldn't have happened if Dougal Douglas hadn't come here," a woman remarked.

He was standing at the altar with Trevor, the best man, behind him. Dixie came up the aisle on the arm of Arthur Crewe, her stepfather. There must have been thirty-odd guests in the church. Arthur Crewe was reported in the papers next day as having said: "I had a feeling the wedding wouldn't come off." At the time he stepped up the aisle with Dixie, tall in her flounces, her eyes dark and open, and with a very little trace round the nose of a cold.

She had said, "Keep away from me. You'll catch my cold, Humphrey. It's bad enough me having a cold for the wedding."

But he said, "I want to catch your cold. I like to think of the germs hopping from you to me."

"I know where you got all these disgusting ideas from. You got them from Dougal Douglas. Well, I'm glad he's gone and there won't be him at the wedding to worry about in case he starts showing off the lumps on his head or something."

"I liked Dougal," Humphrey said.

Here they were, kneeling at the altar. The vicar was reading from the prayer book. Dixie took a lacey handkerchief from her sleeve and gently patted her nose. Humphrey noticed the whiff of scent which came from the handkerchief.

The vicar said to Humphrey, "Wilt thou have this woman to thy wedded wife?"

"No," Humphrey said, "to be quite frank I won't."

He got to his feet and walked straight up the aisle. The guests in the pews rustled as if they were all women. Humphrey got to the door, into his Fiat, and drove off by himself to Folkestone. It was there they had planned to spend their honeymoon.

He drove past the Rye, down Rye Lane roundabout to Lewisham, past the Dutch House and on to Swanley, past Wrotham Hill and along the A20 to Ditton, where he stopped for a drink. After Maidstone he got through the Ashford bypass and stopped again at a pub. He drove on to Folkestone, turning left at the Motel Lympne, where yellow headlamps of the French cars began to appear on the road as they had done before. He stayed in the hotel on the front in the double room booked for the honeymoon, and paid double without supplying explanations to the peering, muttering management.

"Outside," said the barmaid. Humphrey rose, finished his drink with a flourish, regarded his handsome hit face in the mirror behind the barmaid, and followed Trevor Lomas out into the autumn evening, while a woman behind them in the pub remarked, "It wouldn't have happened if Dougal Douglas hadn't come here."

Trevor prepared for a fight, but Humphrey made no move to retaliate; he turned up toward the Rye where his car was parked and where, beside it, Trevor had left his motor-scooter.

Trevor Lomas caught him up. "And you can keep away from round here," he said.

Humphrey stopped. He said, "You after Dixie?"

"What's that to you?"

Humphrey hit him. Trevor hit back. There was a fight. Two courting couples returning from the dusky scope of the Rye's broad lyrical acres stepped to the opposite pavement, leant on the railings by the swimming baths, and watched. Eventually the fighters, each having suffered equal damage to different features of the face, were parted by onlookers to save the intervention of the police.

After Humphrey had been sent away from the door, and the matter had been discussed, Dixie Morse, aged seventeen, daughter of the first G.I. bride to have departed from Peckham and returned, stood in her little room on the upper floor of 12 Rye Grove and scrutinized her savings book. As she counted she exercised her pretty hips, jerking them from side to side to the rhythm of *Pickin' a Chicken*, which tune she hummed.

Her mother came up the stairs. Dixie closed the book and said to her mother through the closed door, ''Quite definitely I'm not taking up with him again. I got my self-respect to think of.''

''Quite right,'' Mavis replied from the other room.

''He wasn't ever the same after he took up with Dougal Douglas,'' Dixie said through the wall.

''I liked Dougal,'' Mavis replied.

''I didn't like him. Trevor didn't like him,'' Dixie said.

Hearing the front-door bell, Dixie stood attentively. Her mother went down and said something to her stepfather. They were arguing as to who should go and answer the door. Dixie went out on the landing and saw her stepbrother Leslie walking along the ground-floor passage in the wrong direction.

''Leslie, open that door,'' Dixie said.

The boy looked up at Dixie. The bell rang again. Dixie's mother burst out of the dim-lit sitting-room.

''If it's him again I'll give him something to remember me by,'' she said, and opened the door. ''Oh, Trevor, it's you, Trevor,'' she said.

''Good evening, Mavis,'' Trevor said.

Dixie returned rapidly to her room to comb her black hair and put on lipstick. When she came down to the sitting-room, Trevor was seated under the standard lamp, between Mavis and her stepfather, waiting for the television play to come to an end. Trevor had a strip of plaster on his face, close to the mouth.

The play came to an end. Mavis rose in her quick way and switched on the central light. Her husband, Arthur Crewe, smiled at everyone, adjusted his coat and offered Trevor a cigarette. Dixie set one leg across the other, and watched the toe of her shoe, which she wriggled.

"You'll never guess who came to the door this evening."

"Humphrey Place," said Trevor.

"You've seen him?"

"Seen him—I've just knocked his head off."

Dixie's stepfather switched off the television altogether, and pulled round his chair to face Trevor.

"I suppose," he said, "you did right."

"*Did* right," said Dixie.

"I *said* did. I didn't say done. Keep your hair on, girl."

Mavis opened the door and called, "Leslie, put the kettle on." She returned with her quick little steps to her chair. "You could have knocked me over," she said. "I was just giving Dixie her tea; it was, I should say, twenty past five and there was a ring at the bell. I said to Dixie, 'Whoever can that be?' So I went to the door, and lo and behold there he was on the doorstep. He said, 'Hallo, Mavis,' he said. I said, 'You just hop it, you.' He said, 'Can I see Dixie?' I said, 'You certainly can't,' I said. I said, 'You're a dirty swine. You remove yourself,' I said, 'and don't show your face again,' I said. He said, 'Come on, Mavis.' I said, 'Mrs. Crewe to you,' and I shut the door in his face." She turned to Dixie and said, "What about making a cup of tea?"

Dixie said, "If he thinks I would talk to him again,

he's making a great mistake. What did he say to you, Trevor?''

Mavis got up and left the room, saying, "If you want anything done in this house you've got to do it yourself."

"Help your mother," said Arthur Crewe absently to Dixie.

"Did he say whether he's gone back to the same job?" Dixie said to Trevor.

Trevor put a hand on each knee and gave a laugh.

Dixie looked from the broad-faced Trevor to the amiable bald head of her stepfather, and started to weep.

"Well, he's come back again," Arthur said. "What you crying for?"

"Don't cry, Dixie," Trevor said.

Dixie stopped crying. Mavis came in with the tea.

Dixie said, "He's common. You only have to look at his sister. Do you know what Elsie did at her first dance?"

"No," said Mavis.

"Well, a fellow came up to her and asked her for a dance. And Elsie said, 'No, I'm sweating.' "

"Well, you never told me that before," Mavis said.

"I only just heard it. Connie Weedin told me."

Trevor gave a short laugh. "We'll run him out of Peckham like we run Dougal Douglas."

"Dougal went of his own accord, to my hearing," Arthur said.

"With a black eye," Trevor said.

Round at the old-fashioned "Harbinger" various witnesses of the fight were putting the story together. The barmaid said: "It was only a few weeks ago. You saw it in the papers. That chap who left the girl at the altar, that's him. She lives up the Grove. Crewe by name."

One landlady out of a group of three said, "No,

she's a Dixie Morse. Crewe's the stepfather. I know because she works at Meadows Meade in poor Miss Coverdale's pool that was. Miss Coverdale told me about her. The fellow had a good position as a refrigerator engineer."

"Who was the chap that hit him?"

"Some friend of the girl's, I daresay."

"Old Lomas's boy. Trevor by name. Electrician. He was best man at the wedding."

"There was I," sang out an old man who was visible with his old wife on the corner bench over in the public bar, "waiting at the church, waiting at the church."

His wife said nothing nor smiled.

"Now then, Dad," the barmaid said.

The old man took a draught of his bitter with a tremble of the elbow and a turn of the wrist.

Before closing time the story had spread to the surrounding public bars, where it was established that Humphrey had called at 12 Rye Grove earlier in the evening.

Even in one of the saloon bars, Miss Connie Weedin heard of the reappearance of Humphrey Place, and the subsequent fight; and she later discussed this at length with her father who was Personnel Manager of Meadows, Meade & Grindley, and at present recovering from a nervous breakdown.

"Dixie's boy has come back," she said.

"Has the Scotch man come back?" he said.

"No, he's gone."

Outside the pub at closing time Nelly Mahone, who had lapsed from her native religion on religious grounds, was at her post the pavement with her long gray hair blown by the late summer wind. There she commented for all to hear, "Praise be to God who employs the weak to confound the strong and whose ancient miracles we see shining even in our times."

Humphrey and Dixie were widely discussed

throughout the rest of the week. The reappearance of the bridegroom was told to Collie Gould, aged eighteen, unfit for National Service, who retold it to the gang at the Elephant; and lastly by mid-morning break at Meadows Meade the occurrence was known to all on the floor such as Dawn Waghorn, cone-winder, Annette Wren, trainee-seamer, Elaine Kent, process-controller, Odette Hill, uptwister, Raymond Lowther, packer, Lucille Potter, gummer; and it was revealed also to the checking department and many of the stackers, the sorters, and the Office.

Miss Merle Coverdale, lately heard of the typing pool, did not hear of it. Mr. Druce, lately Managing Director, did not hear of it. Neither did Dougal Douglas, the former Arts man, nor his landlady Miss Belle Frierne who had known all Peckham in her youth.

But in any case, within a few weeks, everyone forgot the details. The affair is a legend referred to from time to time in the pubs when the conversation takes a matrimonial turn. Some say the bridegroom came back repentant and married the girl in the end. Some say, no, he married another girl, while the bride married the best man. It is wondered if the bride had been carrying on with the best man for some time past. It is sometimes told that the bride died of grief and the groom shot himself on the Rye. It is generally agreed that he answered "No" at his wedding, that he went away alone on his wedding day and turned up again later.

2

Dixie had just become engaged to marry Humphrey when Dougal Douglas joined the firm of Meadows, Meade & Grindley, manufacturers of nylon textiles, a small but growing concern, as Mr. V. R. Druce described it.

At the interview Mr. Druce said to Dougal, "We feel the time has come to take on an Arts man. Industry and the Arts must walk hand in hand."

Mr. Druce had formerly been blond, he was of large build. Dougal, who in the University Dramatics had taken the part of Rizzio in a play about Mary, Queen of Scots, leaned forward and put all his energy into his own appearance; he dwelt with a dark glow on Mr. Druce, he raised his right shoulder, which was already highly crooked by nature, and leaned on his elbow with a becoming twist of the body. Dougal put Mr. Druce through the process of his smile, which was wide and full of white young teeth; he made movements with the alarming bones of his hands. Mr. Druce could not keep his eyes off Dougal, as Dougal perceived.

"I feel I'm your man," Dougal said. "Something told me so when I woke first thing this morning."

"Is that so?" Mr. Druce said. "Is that so?"

"Only a hunch," said Dougal. "I may be wrong."

"Now look," said Mr. Druce, "I must tell you that

we feel we have to see other candidates and can't come to any decision straight away."

"Quite," said Dougal.

At the second interview Mr. Druce paced the floor, while Dougal sat like a monkey-puzzle tree, only moving his eyes to follow Mr. Druce. "You'll find the world of Industry a tough one," Mr. Druce said.

Dougal changed his shape and became a professor. He leaned one elbow over the back of his chair and reflected kindly upon Mr. Druce.

"We are creating this post," said Mr. Druce. "We already have a Personnel Manager, Mr. Weedin. He needs an assistant. We feel we need a man with vision. We feel you should come under Weedin. But you should largely work on your own and find your own level, we feel. Of course you will be under Mr. Weedin."

Dougal leaned forward and became a television interviewer. Mr. Druce stopped walking and looked at him in wonder.

"Tell me," coaxed Dougal, "can you give me some rough idea of my duties?"

"It's up to you, entirely up to you. We feel there's a place for an Arts man to bring vision into the lives of the workers. Wonderful people. But they need vision, we feel. Motion study did marvels in the factory. We had a man from Cambridge advising on motion study. It speeded up our output thirty percent. Movements required to do any given task were studied in detail and he worked out the simplest pattern of movement involving the least loss of energy and time."

"The least loss of energy and time!" Dougal commented.

"The least loss of energy and time," said Mr. Druce. "All our workers' movements are now designed to conserve energy and time in feeding the line. You'll see it on the posters all over the factory, 'Conserve energy and time in feeding the line.' "

"In feeding the line!" Dougal said.

"In feeding the line," Mr. Druce said. "As I say, this expert came from Cambridge. But we felt that a Cambridge man in Personnel wouldn't do. What we feel about you is you'll be in touch with the workers, or rather, as we prefer to say, our staff; you'll be in the know, we feel. Of course you'll find the world of Industry a tough one."

Dougal turned sideways in his chair and gazed out of the window at the railway bridge; he was now a man of vision with a deformed shoulder. "The world of Industry," said Dougal, "throbs with human life. It will be my job to take the pulse of the people and plumb the industrial depths of Peckham."

Mr. Druce said: "Exactly. You have to bridge the gap and hold out a helping hand. Our absenteeism," he said, "is a problem."

"They must be bored with their jobs," said Dougal in a split second of absent-mindedness.

"I wouldn't say bored," said Mr. Druce. "Not bored. Meadows Meade are building up a sound reputation with regard to their worker-staff. We have a training scheme, a recreation scheme, and a bonus scheme. We haven't yet got a pension scheme, or a marriage scheme, or a burial scheme, but these will come. Comparatively speaking we are a small concern, I admit, but we are expanding."

"I shall have to do research," Dougal mused, "into their inner lives. Research into the real Peckham. It will be necessary to discover the spiritual well-spring, the glorious history of the place, before I am able to offer some impetus."

Mr. Druce betrayed a little emotion. "But no lectures on Art," he said, pulling himself together. "We've tried them. They didn't quite come off. The workers, the staff, don't like coming back to the building after working hours. Too many outside attractions. Our aim is to be one happy family."

"Industry is by now," declared Dougal, "a great tradition. Is that not so? The staff must be made conscious of that tradition."

"A great tradition," said Mr. Druce. "That is so, Mr. Douglas. I wish you luck, and I want you to meet Mr. Weedin while you're here." He pressed a button on his desk and, speaking into an instrument, summoned Mr. Weedin.

"Mr. Weedin," he said to Dougal, "is not an Arts man. But he knows his job inside out. Wonderful people, Personnel staff. If you don't tread on his toes you'll be all right with Personnel. Then of course there's Welfare. You'll have some dealings with Welfare, bound to do. But we feel you must find your own level and the job is what you make it— Come in, Mr. Weedin, and meet Mr. Douglas, M.A., who has just joined us. Mr. Douglas has come from Edinburgh to take charge of human research."

If you look inexperienced or young and go shopping for food in the by-streets of Peckham it is as different from shopping in the main streets as it is from shopping in Kensington or the West End. In the little shops in the Peckham by-streets, the other customers take a deep interest in what you are buying. They concern themselves lest you are cheated. Sometimes they ask you questions of a civil nature, such as: Where do you work? Is it a good position? Where are you stopping? What rent do they take off you? And according to your answer they may comment that the money you get is good or the rent you have to pay is wicked, as the case may be. Dougal, who had gone to a small grocer on a Saturday morning, and asked for a piece of cheese, was aware of a young woman with a pram, a middle-aged woman and an old man accumulating behind him. The grocer came to weigh the cheese.

"Don't you give him that," said the young woman; "it's sweating."

"Don't let him give you that, son," said the old man.

The grocer removed the piece of cheese from the scales and took up another.

"You don't want as much as all that," said the older woman. "Is it just for yourself?"

"Only for me," Dougal said.

"Then you want to ask for two ounces," she said. "Give him two ounces," she said. "You just come from Ireland, son?"

"No, Scotland," said Dougal.

"Thought he was Irish from his voice," commented the old man.

"Me too," said the younger woman. "Irish sounds a bit like Scotch like, to hear it."

The older woman said, "You want to learn some experience, son. Where you stopping?"

"I've got temporary lodgings in Brixton. I'm looking for a place round here."

The grocer forgot his grievances and pointed a finger a Dougal.

"You want to go to a lady up on the Rye, name of Frierne. She's got nice rooms; just suit you. All gentlemen. No ladies, she won't have."

"Who's she?" said the young woman. "Don't know her."

"Don't know Miss Frierne?" said the old man.

The older woman said, "She's lived up there all her life. Her father left her the house. Big furniture removers they used to be."

"Give me the address," said Dougal, "and I'll be much obliged."

"I think she charges," said the older woman. "You got a good position, son?"

Dougal leaned on the counter so that his high shoulder heaved higher still. He turned his lean face to answer. "I've just started at Meadows, Meade & Grindley."

"I know them," said the younger woman. "A nice firm. The girl Waghorn works there."

"Miss Frierne's rooms go as high as thirty, thirty-five shillings," remarked the older woman to the grocer.

"Inclusive heat and light," said the grocer.

"Excuse me," said the older woman. "She had meters put in the rooms, that I do know. You can't do inclusive these days."

The grocer looked away from the woman with closed eyes and opened them again to address Dougal.

"If Miss Frierne has a vacancy you'll be a lucky chap," he said. "Mention my name."

"What department you in?" said the old man to Dougal.

"The Office," said Dougal.

"The Office don't get paid much," said the man.

"That depends," the grocer said.

"Good prospects?" said the older woman to Dougal.

"Yes, fine," Dougal said.

"Let him go up Miss Frierne's," said the old man.

"Just out of National Service?" said the older woman.

"No, they didn't pass me."

"That would be his deformity," commented the old man, pointing at Dougal's shoulder.

Dougal nodded and patted his shoulder.

"You was lucky," said the younger woman and laughed a good deal.

"Could I speak to Miss Fergusson?" Dougal said.

The voice at the other end of the line said, "Hold on. I'll see if she's in."

[14]

Dougal stood in Miss Frierne's wood-panelled entrance hall, holding on and looking around him.

At last she came. "Jinny," Dougal said.

"Oh, it's you."

"I've found a room in Peckham. I can come over and see you if you like. How—"

"Listen, I've left some milk boiling on the stove. I'll ring you back."

"Jinny, are you feeling all right? Maria Cheeseman wants me to write her autobiography."

"It will be boiling over. I'll ring you back."

"You don't know the number."

But she had rung off.

Dougal left fourpence on the telephone table and went up to his new room at the very top of Miss Frierne's house.

He sat down among his belongings, which were partly in and partly out of his zipper bag. There was a handsome brass bedstead with a tall railed head along which was gathered a muslin curtain. It was the type of bed which was becoming fashionable again, but Miss Frierne did not know this. It was the only item of furniture in the room for which she had apologized; she had explained it was only temporary and would soon be replaced by a new single divan. Dougal detected in this little speech a good intention, repeated to each newcomer, which never came off. He assured her that he liked the brass bed with its railings and knobs. Could he remove, perhaps, the curtain? Miss Frierne said, no, it needed the bit of curtain, and before long would be replaced by a single divan. But no, Dougal said, I like the bed. Miss Frierne smiled to herself that she had found such an obliging tenant. "Really, I do like it," Dougal said, "more than anything else in the room."

The two windows in the room pleased him, looking

out on a lot of sky and down to Miss Frierne's long lawn and those of her neighbors; beyond them lay the back gardens belonging to the opposite street of houses, but these were neglected, overgrown and packed with junk and sheds for motor-bicycles, not neat like Miss Frierne's and the row of gardens on the near side, with their borders and sometimes a trellis bower.

He saw a little door, four feet high, where the attic ceiling met the wall. He opened it, and found a deep long cupboard using up the remainder of the roof-slope. Having stooped to enter the cupboard, Dougal found he could almost walk in it. He came out, pleased with his fairly useless cave, and started putting away his shirts in the dark painted chest of drawers. He stroked the ceiling, that part of it which sloped down within reach. Some white powdery distemper came off on his fingers. He went downstairs to telephone to Jinny. Her number was engaged.

The linoleum in his room was imitation parquetry and shone with polish. Two small patterned mats and one larger one made islands on the wide floor. Dougal placed a pile of his clothes on each island, then hauled it over the polished floor to the wardrobe. He unlocked his typewriter and arranged his belongings, as all his student-life in Edinburgh Jinny used to do for him. One day in their final year, at Leith docks, watching the boats, she had said: "I must bend over the rails. I've got that indigestion." Already, at this first stage in her illness, he had shown no sympathy. "Jinny, everyone will think you're drunk. Stand up." In the course of her illness she stopped calling him a crooked fellow, and instead became bitter, calling him sometimes a callous swine or a worm. "I hate sickness, not you," he had said. Still, at that time he had forced himself to visit her sometimes in the Infirmary. He got his degree, and was thought of as frivolous in the pubs, not being a Nationalist. Jinny's degree was delayed a year, he meanwhile spending that year in France and finally London, where he lived in Earl's Court and got through his money waiting for Jinny.

For a few weeks he spent much of his time in the flat of the retired actress and singer, Maria Cheeseman, in Chelsea, who had once shared a stage with an aunt of Jinny's.

He went to meet Jinny at last at King's Cross. She had bright high cheek-bones and brown straight hair. They could surely be married in six months' time. "I've to go into hospital again," said Jinny. "I've to have an operation this time. I've a letter to a surgeon in the Middlesex Hospital.

"You'll come and visit me there?" she said.

"No, quite honestly, I won't," Dougal said. "You know how I feel about places of sickness. I'll write to you every day."

She got a room in Kensington, went into hospital two weeks later, was discharged on a Saturday and wrote to tell Dougal not to meet her at the hospital and she was glad he had got the job in Peckham, and was writing Miss Cheeseman's life, and she hoped he would do well in life.

"Jinny, I've found a room in Peckham. I can come over and see you if you like."

"I've left some milk on the stove. I'll ring you back."

Dougal tried on one of his new white shirts and tilted the mirror on the dressing-table to see himself better. Already it seemed that Peckham brought out something in him that Earl's Court had overlooked. He left the room and descended the stairs. Miss Frierne came out of her front room.

"Have you got everything you want, Mr. Douglas?"

"You and I," said Dougal, "are going to get on fine."

"You'll do well at Meadows Meade, Mr. Douglas. I've had fellows before from Meadows Meade."

"Just call me Dougal," said Dougal.

"Douglas," she said, pronouncing it "Dooglass."

"No, *Dougal*—Douglas is my surname."

"Oh, Dougal Douglas. Dougal's the first name."

"That's right, Miss Frierne. What buses do you take for Kensington?"

"It's my one secret weakness," he said to Jinny.

"I can't help it," he said. "Sickness kills me."

"Be big," he said, "be strong. Be a fine woman, Jinny."

"Understand me," he said, "try to understand my fatal flaw. Everybody has one."

"It's time I had my lie-down," she said. "I'll ring you when I'm stronger."

"Ring me tomorrow."

"All right, tomorrow."

"What time?"

"I don't know. Some time."

"You would think we had never been lovers, you speak so coldly," he said. "Ring me at eleven in the morning. Will you be awake by then?"

"All right, eleven." He leaned one elbow on the back of his chair. She was unmoved. He smiled intimately. She closed her eyes.

"You haven't asked for my number," he said.

"All right, leave your number."

He wrote it on a bit of paper and returned south of the river to Peckham. There, as Dougal entered the saloon bar of the "Morning Star," Nelly Mahone crossed the road in her rags crying, "Praise be to the Lord, almighty and eternal, wonderful in the dispensation of all his works, the glory of the faithful and the life of the just." As Dougal bought his drink, Humphrey Place came up and spoke to him. Dougal recalled that Humphrey Place, refrigerator engineer of Freeze-eezy's, was living in the room below his and had been introduced to him by Miss Frierne that morning. Afterward Miss Frierne had told Dougal, "He is clean and go-ahead."

3

"What d'you mean by different?" Mavis said.

"I don't know. He's just different. Says funny things. You have to laugh," Dixie said.

"He's just an ordinary chap," Humphrey said. "Nice chap. Ordinary."

But Dixie could see that Humphrey did not mean it. Humphrey knew that Douglas was different. Humphrey had been talking a good deal about Douglas during the past fortnight and how they sat up talking late at Miss Frierne's.

"Better fetch him here to tea one night," said Dixie's stepfather. "Let's have a look at him."

"He's too high up in the Office," Mavis said.

"He's on research," Dixie said. "He's brainy, supposed to be. But he's friendly, I'll say that."

"He's no snob," said Humphrey.

"He hasn't got nothing to be a snob about," said Dixie.

"*Anything*, not *nothing*."

"Anything," said Dixie, "to be a snob about. He's no better than us just because he's twenty-three and got a good job."

"But he's got to do his overtime for nothing," Mavis said.

"He's the same as what we are," Dixie said.

"You said he was different."

"Well, but no better than us. I don't know why you sit up talking at nights with him."

Humphrey sat up late in Dougal's room.

"My father's in the same trade. He puts himself down as a fitter. Same job."

"It is right and proper," Dougal said, "that you should be called a refrigerator engineer. It brings lyricism to the concept."

"I don't trouble myself about that," Humphrey said. "But what you call a job makes a difference to the Unions. My dad doesn't see that."

"Do you like brass bedsteads?" Dougal said. "We had them at home. We used to unscrew the knobs and hide the fag ends inside."

"By common law," Humphrey said, "a trade union has no power to take disciplinary action against its members. By common law a trade union cannot fine, suspend, or expel its members. It can only do so contractually. That is, by its rules."

"Quite," said Dougal, who was lolling on his brass bed.

"You can use your imagination," Humphrey said. "If a member is expelled from a union that operates a closed shop. . . ."

"Ghastly," said Dougal, who was trying to unscrew one of the knobs.

"But all that won't concern you much," Humphrey said. "What you want to know about for your human research is arbitration in trade disputes. There's the Conciliation Act 1896 and the Industrial Courts Act 1919, but you wouldn't need to go into those. You might study the Industrial Disputes Order 1951. But you aren't likely to have a dispute at Meadows, Meade & Grindley. You might have an issue, though."

"Is there a difference?"

"Oh, a vast difference. Sometimes they take it to law

to decide whether an issue or a dispute has arisen. It's been as far as the Court of Appeal. I'll let you have the books. Issue is whether certain employers should observe certain terms of employment. Dispute is any dispute between employer and employee as to terms of employment or conditions of labor."

"Terrific," Dougal said. "You must have given your mind to it."

"I took a course. But you'll soon get to know what's what in Industrial Relations."

"Fascinating," Dougal said. "Everything is fascinating, to me, so far. Do you know what I came across the other day? An account of the fair up the road at Camberwell Green."

"Fair?"

"According to Colburn's Calendar of Amusements 1840," Dougal said. He reached for his notebook, leaned on his elbow, heaved his high shoulder and read:

There is here, and only here, to be seen what you can see nowhere else, the lately caught and highly accomplished young mermaid, about whom the continental journals have written so ably. She combs her hair in the manner practiced in China, and admires herself in a glass in the manner practiced everywhere. She has had the best instructors in every peculiarity of education, and can argue on any given subject, from the most popular way of preserving plums, down to the necessity of a change of Ministers. She plays the harp in the new effectual style prescribed by Mr. Bocha, of whom we wished her to take lessons, but, having some mermaiden scruples, she begged to be provided with a less popular master. Being so clever and accomplished, she can't bear to be contradicted, and lately leaped out of her tub and floored a distinguished fellow of the Royal Zoological Society, who was pleased to be more curious and cunning than she was pleased to think agreeable. She has composed various poems for the periodicals, and airs with variations for the harp and piano, all very popular and pleasing.

Dougal gracefully cast his books aside. "How I should like to meet a mermaid!" he said.

"Terrific," Humphrey said. "You make it up?" he asked.

"No, I copied it out of an old book in the library. My research. Mendelssohn wrote his *Spring Song* in Ruskin Park. Ruskin lived on Denmark Hill. Mrs. Fitzherbert lived in Camberwell Grove. Boadicea committed suicide on Peckham Rye probably where the bowling green is now, I should imagine. But, look here, how would you like to be engaged to marry a mermaid that writes poetry?"

"Fascinating," Humphrey said.

Dougal gazed at him like a succubus whose mouth is its eyes.

Humphrey's friend, Trevor Lomas, had said Dougal was probably pansy.

"I don't think so," Humphrey had replied. "He's got a girl somewhere."

"Might be versatile."

"Could be."

Dougal said, "The boss advised me to mix with everybody in the district, high and low. I should like to mix with that mermaid."

Dougal put a record on the gramophone he had borrowed from Elaine Kent in the textile factory. It was a Mozart Quartet. He slid the rugs aside with his foot and danced to the music on the bare linoleum, with stricken movements of his hands. He stopped when the record stopped, replaced the rugs, and said, "I must get to know some of the youth clubs. Dixie will be a member of a youth club, I expect."

"She isn't," Humphrey said rather rapidly.

Dougal opened a bottle of Algerian wine. He took his time, and with a pair of long tweezers fished out a bit of cork that had dropped inside the bottle. He held up the pair of tweezers.

"I use these," he said, "to pluck out the hairs which grow inside my nostrils, and which are unsightly. Eventually, I lose the tweezers, then I buy another pair."

He placed the tweezers on the bed. Humphrey lifted them, examined them, then placed them on the dressing table.

"Dixie will know," Dougal said, "about the youth clubs."

"No, she won't. She doesn't have anything to do with youth clubs. There are classes within classes in Peckham."

"Dixie would be upper-working," said Dougal. He poured wine into two tumblers and handed one to Humphrey.

"Well, I'd say middle-class. It's not a snob business, it's a question of your type."

"Or lower-middle," Dougal said.

Humphrey looked vaguely as if Dixie was being insulted. But then he looked pleased. His eyes went narrow, his head lolled on the back of the chair, copying one of Dougal's habitual poses.

"Dixie's saving up," he said. "It's all she can think of, saving up to get marred. And now what does she say? We can't go out more than one night a week so that I can save up too."

"Avarice," Dougal said, "must be her fatal flaw. We all have a fatal flaw. If she took sick, how would you feel, would she repel you?"

* * *

Dougal had taken Miss Merle Coverdale for a walk across the great sunny common of the Rye on a Saturday afternoon. Merle Coverdale was head of the typing pool at Meadows, Meade & Grindley. She was thirty-seven.

Dougal said, "My lonely heart is deluged by melancholy and it feels quite nice."

"Someone might hear you talking like that."

"You are a terror and a treat," Dougal said. "You look to me like an Okapi," he said.

"A what?"

"An Okapi is a rare beast from the Congo. It looks like a deer, but it tries to be a giraffe. It has stripes and it stretches it neck as far as possible and its ears are like a donkey's. It is a little bit of everything. There are only a few in captivity. It is very shy."

"Why do you say I'm like it?"

"Because you're so shy."

"Me shy?"

"Yes. You haven't told me about your love affair with Mr. Druce. You're too shy."

"Oh, that's only a friendship. You've got it all wrong. What makes you think it's a love affair? Who told you that?"

"I've got second sight."

He brought her to the gate of the park and was leading her through it, when she said,

"This doesn't lead anywhere. We'll have to go back the same way."

"Yes, it does," Dougal said, "it leads to One Tree Hill and two cemeteries, the Old and the New. Which would you prefer?"

"I'm not going into any cemetery," she said, standing with legs apart in the gateway as if he might move her by force.

Dougal said, "There's a lovely walk through the New Cemetery. Lots of angels. Beautiful. I'm surprised at you. Are you a free woman or are you a slave?''

She let him take her through the cemetery, eventually, and even pointed out to him the tower of the crematorium when it came into sight. Dougal posed like an angel on a grave which had only an insignificant headstone. He posed like an angel-devil, with his hump shoulder and gleaming smile, and his fingers of each hand widespread against the sky. She looked startled. Then she laughed.

"Enjoying yourself?" she said.

On the way back along the pastoral streets of trees and across the Rye she told him about her six years as mistress of Mr. Druce, about Mr. Druce's wife who never came to the annual dinners and who was a wife in name only.

"How they bring themselves to go on living together I don't know," she said. "There's no feeling between them. It's immoral."

She told Dougal how she had fallen out of love with Mr. Druce yet could not discontinue the relationship, she didn't know why.

"You've got used to him," Dougal said.

"I suppose so."

"But you feel," Dougal said, "that you're living a lie."

"I do," she said. "You've put my very thoughts into words.

"And then," she said, "he's got some funny ways with him."

Dougal slid his eyes to regard her without moving his face. He caught her doing the same thing to him.

"What funny ways? Come on, tell me," Dougal said. "There's no good telling the half and then stopping."

"No," she said. "It wouldn't be right to discuss Mr. Druce with you. He's your boss and mine, after all."

"I haven't seen him," Dougal said, "since the day he engaged me. He must have forgotten about me."

"No, he talked a lot about you. And he sent for you the other day. You were out of the office."

"What day was that?"

"Tuesday. I said you were out on research."

"So I was," said Dougal. "I was out on research."

"Nobody gets forgotten at Meadows Meade," she said. "He'll want to know about your research in a few weeks' time."

Dougal put his long cold hand down the back of her coat. She was short enough for his hand to reach quite a long way. He tickled her.

She wriggled and said, "Not in broad daylight, Dougal."

"In dark midnight," Dougal said, "I wouldn't be able to find my way."

She laughed from her chest.

"Tell me," Dougal said, "what is the choicest of Mr. Druce's little ways?"

"He's childish," she said. "I don't know why I stick to him. I could have left Meadows Meade many a time. I could have got into a big firm. You don't think Meadows Meade's a big firm, do you, by any chance? Because, if you do, let me tell you, Meadows Meade is by comparison very small. Very small."

"It looks big to me," Dougal said. "But perhaps it's the effect of all that glass."

"We used to have open-plan," she said. "So that you could see everyone in the office without the glass, even Mr. Druce. But the bosses wanted their privacy back, so we had the glass partitions put up."

"I like those wee glass houses," Dougal said. "When I'm in the office I feel like a tomato, getting ripe."

"*When* you're in the office."

"Merle," he said, "Merle Coverdale, I'm a hard-working fellow. I've got to be out and about on my human research.''

They were moving up to the Rye where the buses blazed in the sun. Their walk was nearly over.

"Oh, we're soon here," she said.

Dougal pointed to a house on the right. "There's a baby's pram," he said, "stuck out on a balcony which hasn't any railings."

She looked and sure enough there was a pram perched on an open ledge only big enough to hold it, outside a second-floor window. She said, "They ought to be prosecuted. There's a baby in that pram, too."

"No, it's only a doll," Dougal said.

"How do you know?"

"I've seen it before. The house is a baby-carriage works. The pram is only for show."

"Oh, it gave me a fright."

"How long have you lived in Peckham?" he said.

"Twelve and a half years."

"You've never noticed the pram before?"

"No, can't say I have. Must be new."

"From the style of the pram, it can't be new. In fact the pram has been there for twenty-five years. You see, you simply haven't noticed it."

"I don't hardly ever come across the Rye. Let's walk round a bit. Let's go into the Old English garden."

"Tell me more," Dougal said, "about Mr. Druce. Don't you see him on Saturdays?"

"Not during the day. I do in the evening."

"You'll be seeing him tonight?"

"Yes, he comes for supper."

Dougal said, "I suppose he's been doing his garden all day. Is that what he does on Saturdays?"

"No. As a matter of fact, believe it or not, on Saturday mornings he goes up to the West End to the big shops. He goes up and down in the lifts. He rests in the afternoons. Childish."

"He must get some sexual satisfaction out of it."

"Don't be silly," she said.

"A nice jerky lift," said Dougal. "Not one of the new smooth ones but the kind that go yee-oo at the bottom." And Dougal sprang in the air and dipped with bent knees to illustrate his point, so that two or three people in the Old English garden turned to look at him. "It gives me," Dougal said, "a sexual sensation just to think of it. I can quite see the attraction these old lifts have for Mr. Druce. Yee-oo."

She said, "For God's sake lower your voice." Then she laughed her laugh from the chest, and Dougal pulled that blonde front lock of her otherwise brown hair, while she gave him a hefty push such as she had not done to a man for twenty years.

He walked down Nunhead Lane with her; their ways parted by the prefabs at Costa Road.

"I'm to go to tea at Dixie's house tonight," he said.

"I don't know what you want to do with that lot," she said.

"Of course, I realize you're head of the typing pool and Dixie's only a wee typist," he said.

"You're taking me up wrong."

"Let's go for another walk if it's nice on Monday morning," he said.

"I'll be at work on Monday morning. I'll be down to work, not like you."

"Take Monday off, my girl," Dougal said. "Just take Monday off."

"Hallo. Come in. Pleased to see you. There's your tea," Mavis said.

The family had all had theirs, and Dougal's tea was set on the table. Cold ham and tongue and potato salad with bread and butter, followed by fruit cake and tea. Dougal sat down and tucked in while Mavis, Dixie and Humphrey Place sat round the table. When he had fin-

[29]

ished eating, Mavis poured the tea and they all sat and drank it.

"That Miss Coverdale in the pool," said Mavis, "is working Dixie to death. I think she's trying to get Dixie out. Ever since Dixie got engaged she's been horrible to Dixie, hasn't she, Dixie?"

"It was quarter to four," said Dixie, "and she came up with an estimate and said 'priority'—just like that—priority. I said, 'Excuse me, Miss Coverdale, but I've got two priorities already.' She said, 'Well, it's only quarter to four.' 'Only,' I said, 'only quarter to four. Do you realize how long these estimates take? I'm not going without my tea-break, if that's what you're thinking, Miss Coverdale.' She said, 'Oh, Dixie, you're impossible,' and turned away. I jumped up and I said, 'Repeat that,' I said. I said—"

"You should have reported her to Personnel," Humphrey said. "That was your correct procedure."

"A disappointed spinster," Mavis said, "that's what she is."

"She's immoral with Mr. Druce, a married man, that I know for a fact," Dixie said. "So she's covered. You can't touch her, there's no point in reporting her to Personnel. It gets you down."

"Take Monday off," said Dougal. "Take Tuesday off as well. Have a holiday."

"No, I don't agree to that," Humphrey said. "Absenteeism is downright immoral. Give a fair week's work for a fair week's pay."

Dixie's stepfather, who had been watching the television in the sitting-room and who suddenly felt lonely, put his head round the door.

"Want a cup of tea, Arthur?" said Mavis. "Meet Mr. Douglas. Mr. Douglas, Mr. Crewe."

"Where's Leslie?" said Arthur Crewe.

"Well, he ought to be in. I let him go out," Mavis said.

"Because there's something going on out the front," Arthur said.

They all trooped through to the sitting-room and peered into the falling dusk, where a group of young people in their teens were being questioned by an almost equal number of policemen.

"The youth club," Mavis said.

Dougal immediately went out to investigate. As he opened the street door, young Leslie slid in as if from some concealment; he was breathless.

Dougal returned presently to report that the tires of a number of cars parked up at the Rye had been slashed. The police were rounding up the teenage suspects. Young Leslie was chewing bubble-gum. Every now and then he pulled a long strand out of his mouth and let it spring back into his mouth.

"But it seems to me the culprits may have been children," Dougal said, "as much as these older kids."

Leslie stopped chewing for an instant and stared back at Dougal in such disgust that he seemed to be looking at Dougal through his nostrils rather than his eyes. Then he resumed his chewing.

Dougal winked at him. The boy stared back.

"Take that muck out of your mouth, son," said his father.

"You can't stop him," said his mother. "He won't listen to you. Leslie, did you hear what your father said?"

Leslie shifted the gum to the other side of his cheek and left the room.

Dougal looked out of the window at the group who were still being questioned.

"Two girls there come from Meadows Meade," he said. "Odette Hill, uptwister, and Lucille Potter, gummer."

"Oh, the factory lot are always mixed up in the youth club trouble," Mavis said. "You don't want anything to do with that lot.'' As she spoke she moved her hand across her perm, nipping each brown wave in turn between her third and index fingers.

Dougal winked at her and smiled with all his teeth.

Mavis said to Dixie in a whisper, ''Has *he* gone?''

''Yup,'' said Dixie, meaning, yes, her stepfather had gone out for his evening drink.

Mavis went to the sideboard and fetched out a large envelope.

''Here we are again,'' Dixie said.

''She always says that,'' Mavis said.

'Well, Mum, you keep on pulling them out; every new person that comes to the house, out they come.''

Mavis had extracted three large press cuttings from the envelope and handed them to Dougal.

Dixie sighed, looking at Humphrey.

''Why you two not go on out? Go on out to the pictures,'' Mavis said.

''We went out last night.''

''But you didn't go to the pictures, I bet. Saving and pinching to get married, you're losing the best time of your life.''

''That's what I tell her,'' said Humphrey. ''That's what I say.''

''Where'd you go last night?'' Mavis said.

Dixie looked at Humphrey. ''A walk,'' she said.

''What you make of these?'' Mavis said to Dougal.

The cuttings were dated June, 1942. Two of them bore large photographs of Mavis boarding an ocean liner. All announced that she was the first of Peckham's G.I. brides to depart these shores.

''You don't look a day older,'' Dougal said.

''Oh, go on,'' Dixie said.

''Not a day,'' said Dougal. ''Anyone can see your mother's had a romantic life.''

Dixie took her nail file out her bag, snapped the bag shut and started to grate at her nails.

Humphrey bent forward in his chair, one hand on each knee, as if, by affecting intense interest in Mavis's affair, to compensate for Dixie's mockery.

"Well, it was romantic," Mavis said, "and it wasn't. It was both. Glub—that was my first husband—Glub was wonderful at first." Her voice became progressively American. "Made you feel like a queen. He sure was gallant. *And* romantic, as you say. But then . . . Dixie came along . . . everything sorta wenna pieces. We were living a lie," Mavis said, "and it was becoming sorta immoral to live together, not loving each other." She sighed for a space. Then pulling herself together she said, "So I come home."

"*Came* home," Dixie said.

"And got a divorce. And then I met Arthur. Old Arthur's a good sort."

"Mum's had her moments," Dixie said. "She won't let you forget that."

"More than what you'll have, if you go on like you do, putting every penny in the bank. Why, at your age I was putting all my wages what I had left over after paying my keep on my back."

"My own American dad pays my keep," Dixie said.

"He thinks he do, but it don't go far."

"Does. Doesn't," Dixie said.

"I better put the kettle on," Mavis said.

Dougal said then to Dixie, "I didn't never have no money of my own at your age." He heaved his shoulder and glittered his eyes at her, and she did not dare to correct him. But when Humphrey laughed she turned to him and said, "What's the joke?"

"Dougal here," he said, "he's your match."

Mavis came back and switched on the television to a cabaret. Her husband returned to find Dougal keeping the cabaret company with a dance of his own in the middle of their carpet. Mavis was shrieking with joy. Humphrey was smiling with closed lips. Dixie sat also with closed lips, not smiling.

On Saturday mornings, as on Sundays, the gentlemen in Miss Frierne's establishment were desired to make their own beds. On his return at eleven o'clock on Saturday night Dougal found a note in his room.

To-day's bed was a landlady's delight. Full marks in your end-of-term report!

Dougal stuck it up on the mirror of his dressing-table and went downstairs to see if Miss Frierne was still up. He found her in the kitchen, sitting primly up to the table with half a bottle of stout.

"Any letters for me?"

"No, Dougal."

"There should have been a letter."

"Never mind. It might come on Monday."

"Tell me some of your stories."

"You've heard them all, I'm sure." He had heard about the footpads on the Rye in the old days; about the nigger minstrels in the street, or rather carriageway as Miss Frierne said it was called then. She sipped her stout and told him once more of her escapade with a girl called Flo, how they had hired a cab at Camberwell Green and gone up to the Elephant for a drink and treated the cabby to twopenn'orth of gin, and returned without anyone at home being the wiser.

"You must have had some courting days," Dougal said.

But her narrow old face turned away in disdain at the suggestion, for these were early days in their friendship, and it was a full month before Miss Frierne, one evening when she had finished her nourishing stout with a sigh and got out the gin bottle, told Dougal how the Gordon Highlanders were stationed at

Peckham during the first war; how it was a question among the young ladies whether the soldiers wore anything underneath their kilts; how Miss Frierne at the ripe age of twenty-seven went walking with one of the Highlanders up to One Tree Hill; how he turned to her and said, "My girl, I know you're all bloody curious as to what we have beneath the kilt, and I forthwith propose to satisfy your mind on the subject"; how he then took her hand and thrust it under his kilt; and how she then screamed so hard, she had a quinsy for a week.

But in the meantime when Dougal, at the end of his second week at Miss Frierne's, said, "You must have had some courting days," she turned her narrow pale face away from him and indicated by various slight movements of her bony body that he had gone too far.

Eventually she said, "Did Humphrey come in with you?"

"No, I left him round at Dixie's."

"I wanted to ask his private advice about something."

"Anything I can do? I give rare advice."

She was still offended. "No, thank you. I wish to ask Humphrey privately. Do I hear rain?"

Dougal went to bed and the rain danced on the roof above his head. A key clicked in the front door and Humphrey's footsteps, climbing carefully, rose to the first landing. Humphrey paused on the landing, a long pause, as if he were resting from some effort. Then Humphrey's steps fumbled up on the second flight. Either he was drunk or carrying a heavy weight, for he staggered at the top, just outside Dougal's door.

The long cupboard in Dougal's bedroom gave out a loud tom-tom as the rain beat on the low roof within, and together with this sound was discernible that of Humphrey staggering along the short passage to his own room.

Dougal woke again at the very moment, it seemed, that the rain stopped. And at this very moment a whisper and a giggle came from the direction of his cupboard. He switched on his light and got up. The cupboard was empty. Just as he was going to shut the small door again, there was a slight scuffle. He opened the door, put his head in, and found nothing. He returned to bed and slept.

On Monday morning Dougal got his letter. Jinny had finished with him. He went into the offices of Meadows, Meade & Grindley and typed out some of his notes. Then, at the morning tea-break, he walked over to the long, long factory canteen and asked especially for Odette Hill and Lucille Potter. He was told they were not at work that morning. "Taking the day off. Foreman's mad. Absenteeism makes him mad." He had a bun and a cup of tea, then another bun. A bell rang to mark the end of the tea-break. The men disappeared rapidly. A few girls loitered, as on principle, talking with three of the women who served the canteen. Dougal put his head on his arms in full view of these few girls, and wept.

"What's the matter with him?"

"What's the matter, son?" said a girl of about sixteen whom Dougal, on looking up, found to be Dawn Waghorn, one of the cone-winders whose movements when winding the cone, as laid down by the Cambridge expert, had seemed to Dougal, when he had been taken round the floors, very appealing. Dougal put down his head and resumed his weeping.

Dawn patted his poor shoulder. He slightly raised his head and shook it sadly from side to side. A woman came round from the canteen bar with a clean-folded oven cloth which she held out to him. "Here, dry your eyes before anyone sees you," she said.

"What's the matter, mate?" said another girl. She said, "Here's a hanky." She was Annette Wren who was in training for seaming. She was giggling most heartlessly.

"I've lost my girl," Dougal said, as he blew his nose on the oven cloth.

Elaine Kent, who was well on in her twenties, an experienced controller of process, turned on Annette Wren and told her to shut her mouth, what was there to laugh at?

The two other canteen women came round to Dougal, and he was now surrounded by women. Elaine Kent opened her bag and took out a comb. With it she combed Dougal's hair as it moved with his head slowly from side to side.

"You'll get another girl," said one of the canteen women, Milly Lloyd by name.

Annette giggled again. Dawn slapped her face and said, "You're ignorant. Can't you see he's handicapped?"

Whereupon Annette burst into tears.

"Keep your head still," said Elaine. "How can I comb you if you keep moving your head?"

"It calms you down, a good comb," remarked one of the canteen.

Milly Lloyd was looking for a fresh handkerchief for Annette whose sobs were tending toward the hysterical.

"How did you lose your girl?" said Dawn.

"I've got a fatal flaw," Dougal said.

Dawn assumed this to be his deformed shoulder, which she now stroked. "It's a shame," she said. "Little no-good bitch I bet she is."

Suddenly Merle Coverdale appeared at the door in the long distance and started walking toward the group.

"Office," whispered Milly, "typing pool," and returned behind the canteen bar.

Merle shouted along the length of the canteen as she

[37]

approached. "Tea for Mr. Druce, please. He was out. Now he's come in. He wants some tea." Then she saw the group round Dougal. "What the hell's going on?" she said.

"Migraine," Dougal said sadly. "A headache."

"You should all be back on the floor," Merle said to the girls. "There's going to be trouble."

"Who you to talk to us like that?"

"Who's she, coming it over us?"

And so Merle could do nothing with them. She said meaningfully to Dougal,

"I had a headache myself this morning. Came into work late. I went for a brisk walk on the Rye. All by myself."

"I dimly recall arranging to meet you there," Dougal said. "But I was prevented."

Merle gave him a hostile look and said to the canteen women, "What about that tea?"

Milly Lloyd put a cup of tea into Dougal's hand. Merle walked off, bearing Mr. Druce's tea, moving her neck slightly back and forth as she walked all the long length of the canteen. Annette took a cup of tea and, as she gulped it, tried also to express her rage against the girl who had slapped her. As Dougal sipped his tea, young Dawn stroked his high shoulder and said, never mind, it was a shame, while Elaine combed his hair. It was curly hair but cut quite short. Nevertheless she combed it as if it had been as long as the Laughing Cavalier's.

Dixie sat with Humphrey, Dougal and Elaine Kent in Costa's Café. Dixie yawned. Her eyes were sleepy. The only reason she had denied herself an early night was that Dougal was paying for the supper.

"I've felt tired all day," she said. She addressed the men, ignoring Elaine as she had done all evening, because Elaine was factory, even though Elaine was high

[38]

up in process-control. After a trial period Elaine like-wise confined her remarks to the men.

"Look what's just come in," Elaine said. Tall Trevor Lomas had just come in. He sat at the nearest table, with his head and shoulders turned away from Dougal's party, and stared out of the window. Trevor Lomas was at this time employed as an electrician by the Borough.

Trevor turned his head sleepily and permitted an eye to rest on Humphrey for a small second. Humphrey said "Hallo." Trevor did not reply.

Trevor's girl arrived presently, tall and copper-tinted, with a tight short black skirt and much green eye-shadow. "Hi, snake," said Trevor. "Hi," said the girl, and sat down beside him.

Dixie and Elaine stared at the girl as she slid out of her coat and let it fall on the back of her chair. They stared as if by duty, and watched every detail. The girl was aware of this, and seemed to expect it.

Then Trevor pushed back his chair, still seated, so that he half-faced Humphrey's party. He said to his girl in a loud voice: "Got your lace hanky on you, Beauty?"

Beauty did not reply. She was holding up a small mirror, putting on lipstick with care.

"Because," said Trevor, "I'm going to cry." He took his large white handkerchief out of his top pocket and flourished it before each eye in turn. "Going to cry my eyes out, I am," said Trevor, "because I've lost me girl. Hoo, I've lost me girl."

Beauty laughed a great deal. The more she laughed the more noisily did Trevor continue. He laid his head on the table and affected to sob. The girl rocked in her chair, her newly-painted lips open wide apart.

Then Dixie started to laugh.

Dougal shoved his chair back and stood up. Elaine jumped up and held his arm.

"Let be," she said.

Humphrey, whom the story of Dougal's weeping in

[39]

the canteen had not yet reached, said to Dixie, "What's up?"

Dixie could not tell him for laughing.

"Let be, mate," Elaine said to Dougal.

Dougal said to Trevor, "I'll see you up on the Rye outside the tennis court."

Elaine walked over to Trevor and gave him a push. "Can't you see he's deformed?" she said. "Making game of a chap like that, it's ignorant."

Dougal, whose deformed shoulder had actually endowed him with a curious speciality in the art of fighting, in that he was able to turn his right wrist at an extraordinary back-hand outward angle and to get a man by the throat as with a claw, did not at that moment boast of the fact.

"Cripple as I am," he merely said, "I'll knock his mean wee sex-starved conceited low and lying L.C.C. electrician's head off."

"Who's sex-starved?" Trevor said, standing up.

Two youths who had been sitting by the window moved over the better to see. A Greek in an off-white coat appeared, and pointed to a telephone receiver which stuck out of the wall behind him in the passageway to the dim kitchen.

"I'll use that phone," he said.

Trevor gave him one of his long sleepy looks. Then he gave one of them to Dougal.

"Who's sex-starved?" he said.

"You are," Dougal said, while counting his money to pay the bill. "And I'll see you on the Rye within the quarter hour."

Trevor walked out of the café and Beauty hastily wriggled herself into her coat and tripped out after him. After them both went the Greek, but Trevor's motor-scooter had just moved off.

"Hasn't paid for coffee," said the Greek, returning. "What name and address he is, please?"

"No idea," Dougal said. "I don't mix with him."

The Greek turned to Humphrey. "I seen you here before with that fellow."

Humphrey threw half-a-crown on the table, and, as the four departed, the Greek slammed his glass doors behind them as hard as he judged the glass would stand up to.

The two girls got into Humphrey's car, but he at first refused to drive them up to the Rye. Dougal stood and argued on the pavement.

Humphrey said, "No, not at all. Don't go. Don't be a fool, Dougal. Let it pass. He's ignorant."

"All right, I'll walk," Dougal said.

"I'm going to send Trevor Lomas home," Humphrey said. He left Dougal and started up the car and drove off with the girls, Dixie in front and Elaine behind agitating, too late, to be let out.

Dougal arrived at the tennis courts six minutes later. Some seconds before he arrived he had heard a sound as of women screaming.

Between two distant lamp-posts, in their vague oblique light, a group was gathered. Dougal discerned Humphrey and Trevor with a strange youth called Collie who was without a coat and whose shirt was unbuttoned, exposing his chest to the night air. These figures were apparently molesting three further figures who turned out to be Dixie, Elaine, and Beauty, who were screaming. Soon it appeared that the men were not molesting but restraining them. Dixie had a long-strapped shoulder bag with which she was attempting to lay about her, largely in the direction of Elaine. Elaine, who was at present in the grip of Trevor, managed to dig Beauty's leg with her steel stiletto heel. Beauty wailed and struggled in Humphrey's grip.

"What's going on?" Dougal said.

Nobody took any notice of him. He went and hit Trevor in the face. Trevor let go of Elaine so that she fell heavily against Beauty. Meanwhile Trevor hit out at Douglas, who staggered backward into Humphrey. Beauty wailed louder, and struggled harder. Elaine recovered herself and used her freedom to kick with her stiletto heel at Trevor. Dixie, meanwhile, was attempting to release herself from the grasp of that strange youth, Collie, with the bared chest, by biting the arm that held her. The screams grew louder. Dougal's eyes were calculating his chance of coming to adequate terms with Trevor Lomas amidst the confusion when a curious thing happened.

The confusion stopped. Elaine started to sing in the same tone as her screaming, joylessly, and as if in continuation of it. The other girls, seeming to take a signal from her, sidled their wails into a song,

> *Sad to say I'm on my way,*
> *I got a little girl in Kingston Town*

meanwhile casting their eyes fitfully over the Rye beyond the trees.

The strange youth let go of Dixie and began to jive with Elaine. In a few seconds everyone except Dougal was singing, performing the twisting jive, merging the motions of the fight into those of the frantic dance. Dougal saw Humphrey's face as his neck swooped upward. It was frightened. Dixie's expression was, with a decided effort, bright. So was Elaine's. A one-sided smile on the face of the strange boy, and the fact that, as he bent and twisted in the jive, he buttoned up his shirt, made Dougal look round outside the group for the cause of this effect. He saw it immediately. Two policemen were quite close to them now. They must have been observed at a distance of three minutes' police-pace when Elaine had started to sing and the signal had gone round.

"What you think this is—a dance hall?"

"No, constable. No, inspector. Just having a dance with the girls. Just going home, mate."

"Well, *go* home. Get a move on. Out of the park, the lot of you."

"It was Dixie," said Humphrey to Dougal on the way home, "that started the fight. She was over-tired and worked up. She said that tart of Trevor's was giving her looks. She went up to the girl and said, 'Who you looking at?' and then the girl *did* give her a look. Then Dixie let fly with her handbag. That's how it all began."

Rain started to fall as they turned up past the old Quaker cemetery. Nelly Mahone took a green-seeming scarf from a black bag and placed it over her long gray hair. She cried: "The meadows are open and the green herbs have appeared, and the hay is gathered out of the mountain. The wicked man fleeth when no man pursueth, but the just, bold as a lion, shall be without dread."

"Pleasant evening, though a bit wet," Dougal said. Nelly looked round after him.

Up in his room Dougal poured Algerian wine and remarked as he passed a glass to Humphrey,

"The cupboards run the whole length of the attic floor."

Humphrey put the glass on the floor at his feet and looked up at Dougal.

"There was a noise in the cupboard," Dougal said, "the night before last. It went creak-oop, creak-oop. I thought it came from my cupboard here, but I think maybe it didn't. I think maybe it came from your cupboard through the wall. Creak-oop." Dougal bent his knees apart, then sprang up in the air. He repeated this several times. "Creak-oop," he said.

Humphrey said, "It's only on wet Saturday nights when we can't go up on the Rye."

"Isn't she heavy to carry upstairs?" Dougal said.

Humphrey looked alarmed. "Did it sound as if I was carrying her upstairs?"

"Yes. Better to let her walk up in her stocking feet."

"No, she did that once. The old woman came out and nearly caught us."

"Better to lie in the bed than in the creaky cupboard," Dougal said. "The chap in the room below will hear it."

'No, the old woman came up one night when we were in the bed. We were nearly caught. Dixie had to run and hide in the cupboard."

Humphrey lifted his glass of wine from the floor by his feet and drank it in one gulp.

"Don't worry yourself," Dougal said.

"It's a worry what to do. All right on fine Saturday nights; we can go up on the Rye and Dixie gets home about half-past eleven. But if it starts to rain we come back here. I don't see why not, I pay for the room. But there's the difficulty of getting her up, then down again in the morning while the old woman's at early church. Then she has to pay her brother Leslie five shillings a time to let her in quietly. And she worries about that, does Dixie. She's a great saver, is Dixie."

"It's a tiring occupation, is saving," Dougal said. "Dixie's looking tired."

"Yes, as a matter of fact she does lie awake worrying. And there's no need to worry. Terrible at seventeen. I said, 'What you think you'll be like in ten years' time?' "

"When are you getting married?" Dougal said.

"September. Could do before. But Dixie wants a certain sum. She has her mind set to a certain sum. It keeps her awake at night."

"I advised her to take Monday morning off," Dougal said. "Everyone should take Mondays off."

"Now I don't agree to that," Humphrey said. "It's immoral. Once you start absenting yourself you lose your self-respect. *And* you lose the support of your unions; they won't back you. Of course the typists haven't got a union. As yet."

"No?" said Dougal.

[44]

"No," Humphrey said, "but it's a question of principle."

Dougal bent his knees apart as before and leapt into the air. "Creak-oop, creak-oop," he said.

Humphrey laughed deeply with his head thrown back. He stopped when a series of knocks started up from the floor.

"Chap downstairs," Dougal said, "knocks on his ceiling with a broom handle. He doesn't like my wee dances." He performed his antic three times more, shouting, "Creak-oop."

Humphrey cast his head back and laughed, so that Dougal could see the whole inside of his mouth.

"I have a dream at nights," Dougal said, pouring the wine, "of girls in factories doing a dance with only the movements of their breasts, bottoms and arms as they sort, stack, pack, check, cone-wind, gum, uptwist, assemble, seam and set. I see the Devil in the guise of a chap from Cambridge who does motion-study, and he's the choreographer. He sings a song that goes, 'We study in detail the movements requisite for any given task and we work out the simplest pattern of movement involving the least loss of energy and time.' While he sings this song, the girls are waggling and winding, like this—" and Dougal waggled his body and wove his arms intricately. "Like Indian dancing, you know," he said.

"And," said Dougal, "of course this choreographer is a projection of me. I was at the University of Edinburgh myself, but in the dream I'm the Devil and Cambridge."

Humphrey smiled, looked wise, and said, "Inhuman"; which three things he sometimes did when slightly at a loss.

4

Miss Merle Coverdale opened the door of her flat on Denmark Hill, and admitted Mr. Druce in the early evening of midsummer's day. He took off his hat and hung it on a peg in her entrance-hall which was the shape and size of a small kitchen table, and from the ceiling of which hung a crystal chandelier. Mr. Druce followed Merle into the sitting-room. So far he had not spoken, and still without a word, while Merle took up her knitting by the two-bar electric heater, he opened the door of a small sideboard and extracted a bottle of whisky which he lifted up to the light. Opening another compartment of the sideboard he took out a glass. He poured some whisky into it and from a syphon which stood on a tray on the sideboard splashed soda-water into his drink. Then, "Want some?" he said.

"No, thanks."

He sighed and brought his drink to a large chair opposite Merle's smaller one.

"No," she said, "I've changed my mind. I think I feel like a whisky and ginger."

He sighed and went to the sideboard, where, opening a drawer, he extracted a bottle-opener. He stooped to the cupboard and found a bottle of ginger ale.

"No, I'll have gin and tonic. I think I feel like a gin and tonic."

He turned, with the bottle-opener in his hand, and looked at her.

"Yes, I feel like a gin and tonic."

And so he prepared the mixture and brought it to her. Then, sitting down, he took off his shoes and put on a pair of slippers which lay beside the chair.

Presently he looked at his watch. At which Merle put down her knitting and switched on the television. A documentary travel film was in progress, and in accompaniment to this they talked.

"Drover Willis's," he said, "have started on their new extension."

"Yes, you told me the other day."

"I see," he said, "they are advertising for automatic weaver instructors and hands. They are going to do made-up goods as well. They are advertising for ten twin-needle flat-bed machinists, also flat-lock machinists and instructors. They must be expanding."

"Four, five, six," she said, "purl two, seven, eight."

"I see," he said, "they are advertising for an Arts man."

"Well, what do you expect? It was recommended at the Conference, wasn't it?"

"Yes, but remember, Merle, we were the first in the area to adopt that recommendation. Did he come into the office today?"

"No."

"Tell him I want to see him, it's time we had a report. I've only seen him three times since he started. Weedin wants a report."

"Remind me in the morning on the business premises, Vincent," she said. "I don't bring the office into my home, as you know."

"Weedin hasn't seen him for a week. Neither Welfare nor Personnel can get word of him."

She went to clatter dishes in the scullery. Mr. Druce got up and began to lay the table with mats, knives and forks which he took out of the sideboard. Then he went out into the hall and from his coat pocket took a bottle of stomach tablets which he placed on the table together with the pepper and salt.

Merle brought in some bread. Mr. Druce took a bread-knife from the drawer and looked at her. Then he placed the knife beside the bread on the board.

"The Brussels are not quite ready," she said, and she sat in her chair and took up her knitting. He perched on the arm. She pushed him with her elbow in the same movement as she was using for her knitting. He tickled the back of her neck, which she put up with for a while. But suddenly he pinched the skin of her neck. She screamed.

"Sh-sh," he said.

"You hurt me," she said.

"No, I was only doing this." And he pinched her neck again.

She screamed and jumped from the chair.

"The Brussels are ready," she said.

He turned off the television when she brought in the meal. "Bad for the digestion while you're eating," he said.

They did not speak throughout the meal.

Afterward he stood with her in the red-and-white scullery, and looked on while she washed up. She placed the dishes in a red drying-rack while he dried the knives and forks. These he carried into the living-room and put away in their separate compartments in the drawer of the sideboard. As he put away the last fork he watched Merle bring in a tray with coffee cups.

Merle switched on the television and found a play far advanced. They watched the fragment of the play as they drank their coffee. Then they went into the bedroom and took off their clothes in a steady rhythm. Merle took off her cardigan and Mr. Druce took off his coat. Merle went to the wardrobe and brought out a green quilted silk dressing-gown. Mr. Druce went to the wardrobe and found his blue dressing-gown with white spots. Merle took off her blouse and Mr. Druce his waistcoat. Merle put the dressing-gown over her shoulders and, concealed by it, took off the rest of her clothes, with modest gestures. Mr. Druce slid his braces and emerged from his trousers. These he folded carefully and, padding across the room to the window, laid them on a chair. He made another trip bearing his waistcoat and jacket which he placed over the back of the chair.

They stayed in bed for an hour, in the course of which Merle twice screamed because Mr. Druce had once pinched and once bit her. "I'm covered with marks as it is," she said.

Mr. Druce rose first and put on his dressing-gown. He went to wash and return very soon, putting a wet irritable hand round the bedroom door. Merle said, "Oh, isn't there a towel?" and taking a towel from a drawer, placed it in his hand.

When he returned she was dressed.

She went into the scullery and put on the kettle while he put on his trousers and went home to his wife.

A western breeze blew over the Rye and it was midsummer night, a Saturday. Humphrey carried the two tartan rugs from his car while Dixie walked by his side, looking to left and right and sometimes turning to see if the path was clear of policemen.

Dixie said, "I'm cold."

He said, "It's a warm night."

She said, "I'm cold."

He said, "We've got two rugs."

She walked on beside him until they came to their usual spot under a tree behind the hedge of the Old English garden.

Humphrey spread a rug and she sat down upon it. She lifted the fringe and started to pull at it, separating the matted threads.

He spread the other rug over her legs and lay leaning on his elbow beside her.

"My mum got suspicious the other night," she said. "Leslie told her I was stopping over Camberwell after the dance with Connie Weedin, but she got suspicious. And when I got in she asked me all sorts of questions about the dance. I had to make them up."

"Sure you can trust Leslie?"

"Well, I give him five shillings a week. I think it should be three shillings weeks when I don't stop out all night. But he's greedy, Leslie is."

Humphrey pulled her toward him, and started to unbutton her coat. She buttoned it up again. "I'm cold," she said.

"Oh, come on, Dixie," he said.

"Connie Weedin got an increment," she said. "I've got to wait for my increment till August. I only found out through the girl that does the copy die-stamp operation and had the staff salaries' balance sheet to do. Connie Weedin does the same job as what I do and she's only been there six months longer. It's only because her father's Personnel. I'm going to take it up with Miss Coverdale."

Humphrey pulled her down toward him again and kissed her face.

"What's the matter?" he said. "There's something the matter with you."

"I'm going to take Monday off," she said. "They appreciate you more if you stop away now and again."

"Well, frankly and personally," Humphrey said, "I think it's an immoral thing to do."

"Fifteen shillings rise, less tax, nine and six in Connie Weedin's packet," she said, "and I've got to wait to August. And they're all in it together. And if I don't get satisfaction from Miss Coverdale, who is there to go to? Only Personnel, and that's *Mr.* Weedin. Naturally he's going to cover up for his daughter. And if I go above him to Mr. Druce he'll only send me back to Miss Coverdale, because you know what's between *them*."

"When we're married you won't have to worry about any of them. We can get married Saturday week if you like."

"No, I don't like. What about the house? There's got to be money down for the house."

"There's money down for the house," he said.

"What about my spin-dryer?"

"Oh, to hell with your spin-dryer."

"That fifteen shillings less tax that's due to me," she said, "could have gone in the bank. If it's due to her it's due to me. Fair's fair."

He pulled the top rug up to her chin and under it started to unbutton her coat.

She sat up.

"There's something wrong with you," he said. "We should have gone dancing instead. It wouldn't have cost much."

"You're getting too sexy," she said. "It's through you having to do with Dougal Douglas. He's a sex maniac. I was told. He's immoral."

"He isn't," Humphrey said.

"Yes he is, he talks about sex quite open, any time of the day. Girls and sex."

"Why don't you relax like you used to do?" he said.

"Not unless you give up that man. He's putting ideas in your head."

"You've done plenty yourself to put ideas in my head," he said. "I didn't used to need to look far to get ideas, when you were around. Especially up in the cupboard."

"Repeat that, Humphrey."

"Lie down and relax."

"Not after what you said. It was an insult."

"I know what's the matter with you," he said. "You're losing all your sex. It's all this saving up to get married and looking to the lolly all the time, it takes the sex out of a girl. It stands to reason, it's only psychological."

"You must have been talking it over with Dougal Douglas," she said. "You wouldn't have thought of that by yourself."

She stood up and brushed down her coat. He folded up the rugs.

"I won't be talked about, it's a let-down," she said.

"Who's talked about you?" he said.

"Well, if you haven't talked about me, you've been listening to *him* talking."

"Let me tell you something," he said. "Dougal Douglas is an educated man."

"My mum's uncle's a teacher and he doesn't act like him. He doesn't cry his eyes out like Dougal did in our canteen." Dixie laughed. "He's a pansy."

"That's just his game. You don't know Dougal. I bet he wasn't crying really."

"Yes, he was. He only just lost his girl, and he cried like anything. Make you laugh."

"Then he can't be a pansy, or he wouldn't cry over a girl."

"He must be or he wouldn't cry at all."

On midsummer night Trevor Lomas walked with a somnambulistic sway into Findlater's Ballroom and looked round for Beauty. The floor was expertly laid and polished. The walls were pale rose, with concealed lighting. Beauty stood on the girls' side, talking to a group of very similar and lustrous girls. They had prepared themselves for this occasion with diligence, and as they spoke together, they did not smile much nor attend to each other's words. As an accepted thing, any of the girls might break off in the middle of a sentence, should a young man approach her, and, turning to him, might give him her entire and smiling regard.

Most of the men looked as if they had not properly woken from deep sleep, but glided as if drugged, and with half-closed lids, toward their chosen partner. This approach found favor with the girls. The actual invitation to dance was mostly delivered by gesture; a scarcely noticeable flick of the man's head toward the dance floor. Whereupon the girl, with an outstretched movement of surrender, would swim into the hands of the summoning partner.

Trevor Lomas so far departed from the norm as to indicate to Beauty his wish by word of mouth, which he did not, however, open more than a sixteenth of an inch.

"Come and wriggle, Snake," he said through this aperture.

Findlater's rooms were not given to rowdy rock but concentrated instead upon a more cultivated jive, cha-cha and variants. Beauty wriggled with excellence, and was particularly good at shrugging her shoulders and lifting forward her small stomach; while Trevor's knee-work was easy. Dougal, who had just entered with blonde Elaine, looked round with approval.

During the next dance—forward half a step, one fall and a dip, back half a step, one fall and a dip—Beauty flicked her lashes toward the bandleader who was then facing the dancers, a young pale man with a thin neck which sprouted from a loose jacket of sky-blue. He acknowledged the gesture with one swift rise-and-drop of the eyebrows. Trevor looked round at the man who had now turned to his band and was flicking his limp wrists very slightly. Trevor's teeth said, "Who's your friend?"

"Whose friend?"

The crown of Trevor's head briefly indicated the band-leader.

Beauty shrugged in her jive and expressed her reply, both in the same movement.

Dougal was dancing with Elaine. He leapt into the air, he let go her hands and dangled his arms in front of his hunched body. He placed his left hand on his hip and raised his right while his feet performed the rapid movements of the Highland Fling, heel to instep, then to knee. Elaine bowed her body and straightened it again and again in her laughter. The jiving couples slowed down like an unwound toy roundabout, and gathered beside Dougal. A tall stout man in evening dress walked over to the band; he said something to the band-leader who looked over his shoulder, observed the crowd round Dougal, and stopped the band.

"Hooch!" cried Dougal as the band stopped.

Everyone was talking or laughing. Those who were talking were all saying the same thing. They either said, "Tell him to take more water in it," or "Shouldn't be allowed," or "He's all right. Leave him alone." Some clapped their hands and said, " 'Core." The tall stout manager came over to Dougal and said with a beaming face, "It's all right, son, but no more, please."

"Don't you like Highland dancing?" Dougal said.

The manager beamed and walked away. The band started up. Dougal left the hall followed by Elaine. He reappeared shortly with Elaine tugging his arm in the opposite direction. However, he pressed into the midst of the dancers, bearing before him the lid of a dustbin, which he had obtained from the back premises. Then he placed the lid upside down on the floor, sat cross-legged inside it, and was a man in a rocking boat rowing for his life. The band stopped, but nobody noticed the fact, owing to the many different sounds of mirth, protest, encouragement and rage. The dancers circled slowly around him while he performed a Zulu dance with the lid for a shield.

Two West Indians among the crowd started to object.

"No, man."

"We don't take no insults, man."

But two other tall, black and shining dancers cheered him on, bending at the knees and clapping. These were supported by their woolly-cropped girls who laughed loud above the noise, rolling their bodies from the waist, rolling their shoulders, heads and eyes.

Dougal bowed to the black girls.

Next, Dougal sat on his haunches and banged a message out on a tom-tom. He sprang up and with the lid on his head was a Chinese coolie eating melancholy rice. He was an ardent cyclist, crouched over handlebars and pedalling uphill with the lid between his knees. He was an old woman with an umbrella; he stood on the upturned edges of the lid and speared fish from his rocking canoe; he was the man at the wheel of a racing car; he did many things with the lid before he finally propped the dust-bin lid up on his high shoulder, beating this cymbal rhythmically with his hand while with the other hand he limply conducted an invisible band, being, with long blank face, the band-leader.

The manager pushed through the crowd, still beaming. And, still beaming, he pointed out that the lid was scratching and spoiling the dance floor, and that Dougal had better leave the premises. He took Dougal, who still bore the dust-bin lid, by the elbow.

"Don't you get rough with him," Elaine shouted. "Can't you see he's deformed?"

Dougal disengaged his elbow from the manager's grasp and himself took the manager by the elbow.

"Tell me," Dougal said, as he propelled the manager through the door, "have you got a fatal flaw?"

[55]

"It's the best hall in South London and we don't want it mucked up, see? If we put on a cabaret we do it properly."

"Be kind enough," Dougal said, "to replace this lid on the dust-bin out yonder while I return to the scene within."

Elaine was standing behind him. "Come and leap, leopard," Dougal said, and soon they were moving with the rest.

They were passed by Trevor and Beauty. Trevor regarded Dougal from under his lids, letting the corners of his mouth droop meaningfully.

"Got a pain, panda?" Dougal said.

"Now, don't start," Elaine said.

Beauty laughed up and down the scale as she wriggled.

When Trevor passed again he said to Dougal, "Got your lace hanky on you?"

Dougal put out his foot. Trevor stumbled. The band started playing the National Anthem. Trevor said, "You ought to get a surgical boot and lift your shoulder up to line."

"Have respect for the National Anthem," Beauty said. Her eyes were on the band-leader who, as he turned to face the floor, raised his eyebrows slightly in her direction.

"See you up on the Rye," Dougal said.

Elaine said, "Oh, no, you don't. You're seeing me home."

Trevor said, "You girls got to go home together. I've got a date with a rat on the Rye."

Several of the dancers, as they left the hall, called out to Dougal various words of gratitude, such as, "Thanks a lot for the show" and "You was swell, boy."

Dougal bowed.

Beauty, on her way to the girls' cloakroom, loitered

[56]

a little behind the queue. The band-leader passed by her and moved his solemn lips very slightly. Trevor, close by, heard him say, "Come and frolic, lamb."

Beauty moved her eyes to indicate the presence of Trevor, who observed the gesture.

"She's going straight home," Trevor said through his nose, putting his face close to that of the band-leader. He gave Beauty a shove in the direction of the queue.

Beauty immediately turned back to the band-leader. "No man," she said to Trevor, "lays hands on me."

The band-leader raised his eyebrows and dropped them sadly.

"You're coming home with me," Trevor told her.

"Thought you got a date on the Rye."

"He'll keep," Trevor said.

Beauty took a mirror from her bag and carefully applied her lipstick, turning her bronze head from side to side as she did so. Meanwhile her eyes traced the band-leader's departure from the hall.

"Elaine and I's going home together," she said.

"No, you don't," Trevor said. He peered out to the crowded entrance and there saw Elaine hanging on to Dougal. He caught her attention and beckoned to her by moving his forefinger twice very slowly. Elaine disengaged her arm from Dougal's, opened her bag, took out a cigarette, lit it, puffed slowly, then ambled over to Trevor.

"If you know what's good for your friend you'll take him home," Trevor said.

Elaine blew a puff of smoke in his face and turned away.

"The fight's off," she said to Dougal when she rejoined him. "He wants to keep an eye on his girl, he don't trust her. She got no morals."

As Trevor and Beauty emerged from the hall, Dougal, on the pavement, said to him, "Feeling frail, nightingale?"

Trevor shook off Beauty's arm and approached Dougal.

"Now don't start with him," Elaine shrieked at Dougal, "he's ignorant."

Beauty walked off on her own, with her high determined heels and her model-girl sway, placing her feet confidently and as on a chalk line.

Trevor looked round after her, then ran and caught her up.

Dougal walked with Elaine to Camberwell Green where, standing under the orange lights, he searched his pockets. When he had found a folded sheet of paper he opened it and read, " 'I walked with her to Camberwell Green, and we said goodbye rather sorrowfully at the corner of New Road; and that possibility of meek happiness vanished for ever.' This is John Ruskin and his girl Charlotte Wilkes," Dougal said, "my human research. But you and I will not say goodbye here and now. No. I'm taking you the rest of the way home in a taxi, because you're the nicest wee process-controller I've ever met."

"One thing about you I'll admit," she said, "you're different. If I didn't know you were Scotch I'd swear you were Irish. My mother's Irish."

She said they could not take a taxi up to her door because her mother didn't like her coming home with men in taxis. They dropped off at the Canal Head at Brixton.

"I'm leaving Meadows Meade," Elaine said, "Saturday week. Starting on the Monday at Drover Willis's. It's advancement."

"I saw they were advertising," Dougal said, "for staff at Drover Willis's."

They walked along by the Canal a little way, watching the quiet water.

❧ 5 ❧

Mr. Druce said with embarrassment, "I feel I should just mention the fact that absenteeism has increased in the six weeks you've been with us. Eight percent to be precise. Not that I'm complaining. I'm not complaining. Rome can't be built in a day. I'm just mentioning a factor that Personnel keep stressing. Weedin's a funny sort of fellow. How do you find Weedin?"

"Totally," Dougal said, "lacking in vision. It is his fatal flaw. Otherwise quite sane." He bore on his uneven shoulders all the learning and experience of the world as he said it. Mr. Druce looked away, looked again at Dougal, and looked away.

"Vision," said Mr. Druce.

"Vision," Dougal said, and he was a confessor in his box, leaning forward with his insidious advice through the grille, "is the first requisite of sanity."

"Sanity," Mr. Druce said.

Dougal closed his eyes and slowly smiled with his wide mouth. Dougal nodded his head twice and slowly, as one who understands all. Mr. Druce was moved to confess, "Sometimes I wonder if I'm sane myself, what with one thing and another." Then he laughed and said, "Fancy the Managing Director of Meadows, Meade & Grindley saying things like this."

Dougal opened his eyes. "Mr. Druce, you are not as happy as you might be."

"No," Mr. Druce said, "I am not. Mrs. Druce, if I may speak in confidence . . ."

"Certainly," Dougal said.

"Mrs. Druce is not a wife in any real sense of the word."

Dougal nodded.

"Mrs. Druce and I have nothing in common. When we were first married thirty-two years ago I was a travelling salesman in rayon. Times were hard, then. But I got on." Mr. Druce looked pleadingly at Dougal. "I was a success. I got on."

Dougal tightened his lips prudishly, and nodded, and he was a divorce judge suspending judgment till the whole story was heard out.

"You can't get on in business," Mr. Druce pleaded, "unless you've got the fiber for it.

"You can't get on," Mr. Druce said, "unless you've got the moral fiber. *And* you don't have to be narrow-minded. That's one thing you don't have to be."

Dougal waited.

"You have to be broad-minded," Mr. Druce protested. "In this life." He laid his elbow on the desk and, for a moment, his forehead on his hand. Then he shifted his chin to his hand and continued, "Mrs. Druce is not broad-minded. Mrs. Druce is narrow-minded."

Dougal had an elbow on each arm-rest of his chair, and his hands were joined under his chin. "There is some question of incompatibility, I should say," Dougal said. "I should say," he said, "you have a nature at once deep and sensitive, Mr. Druce."

"Would you really?" Druce inquired of the analyst.

"And a sensitive nature," Dougal said, "requires psychological understanding."

"My wife," Druce said, ". . . it's like living a lie. We don't even speak to each other. Haven't spoken for nearly five years. One day, it was a Sunday, we have having lunch. I was talking away quite normally;

you know, just talking away. And suddenly she said, 'Quack, quack.' She said, 'Quack, quack.' She said, 'Quack, quack,' and her hand was opening and shutting like this—'' Mr. Druce opened and shut his hand like a duck's bill. Dougal likewise raised his hand and made it open and shut. ''Quack, quack,'' Dougal said. ''Like that?''

Mr. Druce dropped his arm. ''Yes, and she said, 'That's how *you* go on—quack, quack.' ''

''Quack,'' Dougal said, still moving his hand, ''quack.''

''She said to me, my wife,'' said Mr. Druce, ''she said, 'That's how *you* go quacking on.' Well, from that day to this I've never opened my mouth to her. I can't, Dougal, it's psychological, I just can't—you don't mind me calling you Dougal?''

''Not at all, Vincent,'' Dougal said. ''I feel I understand you. How do you communicate with Mrs. Druce?''

''Write notes,'' said Mr. Druce. ''Do you call that a marriage?'' Mr. Druce bent to open a lower drawer of his desk and brought out a book with a bright yellow wrapper. Its title was *Marital Relational Psychology.* Druce flicked over the pages, then set the book aside. ''It's no use to me,'' he said. ''Interesting case histories but it doesn't cover my case. I've thought of seeing a psychiatrist, and then I think, why should I? Let *her* see a psychiatrist.''

''Take her a bunch of flowers,'' Dougal said, looking down at the back of his hand, the little finger of which was curling daintily. ''Put your arms around her,'' he said, becoming a lady-columnist, ''and start afresh. It frequently needs but one little gesture from one partner—''

''Dougal, I can't. I don't know why it is, but I can't.'' Mr. Druce placed a hand just above his stomach. ''Something stops me.''

[61]

"You two must separate," Dougal said, "if only for a while."

Mr. Druce's hand abruptly removed from his stomach. "No," he said, "oh, no, I can't leave her." He shifted in his chair into his businesslike pose. "No, I can't do that. I've got to stay with her for old times' sake."

The telephone rang. "I'm engaged," he said sharply into it. He jerked down the receiver and looked up to find Dougal's forefinger pointing into his face. Dougal looked grave, lean and inquisitorial. "Mrs. Druce," Dougal said, "has got money."

"There are interests in vital concerns which we both share," Mr. Druce said with his gaze on Dougal's finger, "Mrs. Druce and I."

Dougal shook his outstretched finger a little. "She won't *let* you leave her," he said, "because of the money."

Mr. Druce looked frightened.

"And there is also the information which she holds," Dougal said, "against you."

"What are you talking about?"

"I'm fey. I've got Highland blood." Dougal dropped his hand. "You have my every sympathy, Vincent," he said.

Mr. Druce laid his head on his desk and wept.

Dougal sat back and lit a cigarette out of Mr. Druce's box. He heaved his high shoulder in a sigh. He sat back like an exhausted medium of the spiritualist persuasion. "Does you good," Dougal said, "a wee greet. A hundred years ago all chaps used to cry regardless."

Merle Coverdale came in with the letters to be signed. She clicked her heels together as she stopped at the sight.

"Thank you, Miss Coverdale," Dougal said, putting out a hand for the letters.

Meanwhile Mr. Druce sat up and blew his nose.

[62]

"Got a comb on you?" Dougal said, squeezing Merle's hand under the letters.

She said, "This place is becoming chaos."

"What was that, Miss Coverdale?" Mr. Druce said with as little moisture as possible.

"Mr. Druce has a bad head," Dougal said as he left the room with her.

"Come and tell me what happened," said Merle.

Dougal looked at his watch. "Sorry, can't stop. I've got an urgent appointment in connection with my human research."

Dougal sat in the cheerful waiting-room looking at the tulips in their earthy bowls.

"Mr. Douglas Dougal?"

Dougal did not correct her. On the contrary he said, "That's right."

"Come this way, please."

He followed her into the office of Mr. Willis, managing director of Drover Willis's, textile manufacturers of Peckham.

"Good afternoon, Mr. Dougal," said the man behind the desk. "Take a seat."

On hearing Mr. Willis's voice Dougal changed his manner, for he perceived that Mr. Willis was a Scot.

Mr. Willis was looking at Dougal's letter of application.

"Graduate of Edinburgh?" said Mr. Willis.

"Yes, Mr. Willis."

Mr. Willis's blue eyes stared out of his brick-colored small-featured face. They stared and stared at Dougal.

"Douglas Dougal," the man read out from Dougal's letter, and asked with a one-sided smile, "Any relation to Fergie Dougal the golfer?"

"No," Dougal said. "I'm afraid not."

Mr. Willis smiled by turning down the sides of his mouth.

"Why do you want to come into Industry, Mr. Dougal?"

"I think there's money in it," Dougal said.

Mr. Willis smiled again. "That's the correct answer. The last candidate answered, 'Industry and the Arts must walk hand in hand,' when I put that question to him. His answer was wrong. Tell me, Mr. Dougal, why do you want to come to us?"

"I saw your advertisement," Dougal said, "and I wanted a job. I saw your advertisements, too, for automatic weaver instructors and hands, and for twin-needle flat-bed machinists and flat-lock machinists and instructors. I gathered you're expanding."

"You know something about textiles?"

"I've seen over a factory. Meadows, Meade & Grindley."

"Meadows Meade are away behind us."

"Yes. So I gathered."

"Now I'll tell you what we're looking for, what we want. . . ."

Dougal sat upright and listened, only interrupting when Mr. Willis said, "The hours are nine to five-thirty."

"I would need time off for research."

"Research?"

"Industrial relations. The psychological factors behind the absenteeism, and so on, as you've been saying—"

"You could do an evening course in industrial psychology. And of course you'd have access to the factory."

"The research I have in mind," Dougal said, "would need the best part of the day for at least two months. Two months should do it. I want to look into the external environment. The home conditions. Peckham must have a moral character of its own."

Mr. Willis's blue eyes photographed every word.

Dougal sat out these eyes, he went on talking, reasonably, like a solid steady Edinburgh boy, all the steadier for the hump on his shoulder.

"I'll have to speak to Davis. He is Personnel. We have to talk over the candidates and we may ask to see you again, Mr. Dougal. If we decide on you, don't fear you'll be hampered in your research."

The factory was opening its gates as Dougal came down the steps from the office into the leafy lanes of Nun Row. Some of the girls were being met by their husbands and boy friends in cars. Others rode off on motor-scooters. A number walked down to the station. "Hi, Dougal," called one of them, "what you doing here?"

It was Elaine, who had now been over a week at Drover Willis's.

"What you doing here, Dougal?"

"I'm after a job," he said. "I think I've got it."

"You leaving Meadows Meade too?"

"No," he said, "oh, no, not on your life."

"What's your game, Dougal?"

"Come and have a drink," he said, "and my Christian name is Douglas on this side of the Rye, mind that. Dougal Douglas at Meadows Meade and Douglas Dougal at Willis's, mind. Only a formality for the insurance cards and such."

"I better call you Doug, and be done with it."

Dixie sat at her desk in the typing pool and, without lifting her eyes from her shorthand book or interrupting the dance of her fingers on the keyboard, spoke out her reply to her neighbor.

"He's all one-sided at the shoulders. I don't know how any girl could go with him."

Connie Weedin, daughter of the Personnel Manager, typed on and said, "My Dad says he's nuts. But I say he's got something. Definitely."

"Got something, all right. Got a good cheek. My

young brother doesn't like him. My mum likes him. My dad likes him so-so. Humphrey likes him. I don't agree to that. The factory girls like him—what can you expect? I don't like him, he's got funny ideas." She stopped typing with her last word and took the papers out of her typewriter. She placed them neatly on a small stack of papers in a tray, put an envelope in her typewriter, typed an address, put more papers in her typewriter, turned over the page of her shorthand notes, and started typing again. "My dad doesn't mind him, but Leslie can't stand him. I tell you who else doesn't like him."

"Who?"

"Trevor Lomas. Trevor doesn't like him."

"I don't like Trevor, never did," Connie said. "Definitely ignorant. He goes with that girl from Celia Modes that's called Beauty. Some beauty!"

"He's a good dancer. He doesn't like Dougal Douglas and, boy, I'll say he's got something there," Dixie said.

"My dad says he's nuts. Supposed to be helping my dad to keep the factory sweet. But my dad says he don't do much with all his brains and his letters. But you can't help but like him. He's different."

"He goes out with the factory girls. He goes out with Elaine Kent that was process-controller. She's gone to Drover Willis's. He goes out with her ladyship too."

"You don't say?"

"I do say. He better watch out for Mr. Druce if it's her ladyship he's after."

"Watch out—her ladyship's looking this way."

Miss Merle Coverdale, at her supervisor's seat at the top of the room, called out, "Is there anything you want, Dixie?"

"No."

"If there's anything you want, come and ask. Is there anything you want, Connie?"

"No."

"If there's anything you want, come up here and ask for it."

Dougal came in just then, and walked with his springy step all up the long open-plan office, bobbing as he walked as if the plastic inlay flooring was a certain green and paradisal turf.

"Good morning, girls."

"You'd think he was somebody," Dixie said.

Connie opened a drawer in her small desk in which she kept a mirror, and looking down into it, tidied her hair.

Dougal sat down beside Merle Coverdale.

"There was a personal call for you," she said, handing him a slip of paper, "from a lady. Will you ring this number?"

He looked at it, put the paper in his pocket and said, "One of my employers."

Merle gave one of her laughs from the chest. "Employers—that's a good name for them. How many you got?"

"Two," Dougal said, "and a possible third. Is Mr. Weedin in?"

"Yes, he's been asking for you."

Dougal jumped up and went in to Mr. Weedin where he sat in one of the glass offices which extended from the typing pool.

"Mr. Douglas," said Mr. Weedin, "I want to ask you a personal question. What do you mean exactly by vision?"

"Vision?" Dougal said.

"Yes, vision, that's what I said."

"Do you speak literally as concerning optics, or figuratively, as it might be with regard to an enlargement of the total perceptive capacity?"

"Druce is complaining we haven't got vision in this department. I thought perhaps maybe you had been having one of your long chats with him."

"Mr. Weedin," Dougal said, "don't tremble like that.

Just relax." He took from his pocket a small square silver vinaigrette which had two separate compartments. Dougal opened both lids. In one compartment lay some small white tablets. In the other were a number of yellow ones. Dougal offered the case to Mr. Weedin. "For calming down you take two of the white ones and for revving up you take one of the yellow ones."

"I don't want your drugs. I just want to know—"

"The yellow ones make you feel sexy. The white ones, being of a relaxing nature, ensure the more successful expression of such feelings. But these, of course, are mere by-effects."

"Do you want my job? Is that what you're wanting?"

"No," Dougal said.

"Because if you want it you can have it. I'm tired of working for a firm where the boss listens to the advice of any young showpiece that takes his fancy. I've had this before. I had it with Merle Coverdale. She told Druce I was inefficient at relationship-maintenance. She told Druce that everything in the pool goes back to me through my girl Connie. She—"

"Miss Coverdale is a sensitive girl. Like an Okapi, you know. You spell it OKAPI. A bit of all sorts of beast. Very rare, very nervy. You have to make allowances."

"And now you come along and you tell Druce we lack vision. And Druce calls me in and I see from the look on his face he's got a new idea. Vision, it is, this time. Try to take a tip or two, he says, from the Arts man. I said, he never hardly puts a foot inside the door does your Arts man. Nonsense, Weedin, he says, Mr. Douglas and I have many long session. He says, watch his manner, he has a lovely manner with the workers. I said, yes, up on the Rye Saturday nights. That is unworthy of you, Weedin, he says. Is it coincidence, says I, that absenteeism has risen eight percent since Mr. Douglas came here and is still rising? Things are bound to get worse, he says, before they get better. If you had the vision, Weedin, he says, you would comprehend my meaning. Study Douglas, he says, watch his methods."

"Funny thing I've just found out," Dougal said, "we have five cemeteries up here round the Rye within the space of a square mile. We have Camberwell New, Camberwell Old—that's full up. We have Nunhead, Deptford and Lewisham Green. Did you know that Nunhead reservoir holds twenty million gallons of water? The original title that Mendelssohn gave his *Spring Song* was *Camberwell Green*. It's a small world."

Mr. Weedin laid his head in his hand and burst into tears.

Dougal said, "You're a sick man, Mr. Weedin. I can't bear sickness. It's my fatal flaw. But I've brought a comb with me. Would you like me to comb your hair?"

"You're unnatural," said Mr. Weedin.

"All human beings who breathe are a bit unnatural," Dougal said. "If you try to be too natural, see where it gets you."

Mr. Weedin blew his nose, and shouted at Dougal: "It isn't possible to get another good position in another firm at my age. Personnel is a much-coveted position. If I had to leave here, Mr. Douglas, I would have to take a subordinate post elsewhere. I have my wife and family to think of. Druce is impossible to work for. It's impossible to leave this firm. Sometimes I think I'm going to have a breakdown."

"It would not be severe in your case," Dougal said. "It is at its worst when a man is a skyscraper. But you're only a nice wee bungalow."

"We live in a flat," Mr. Weedin managed to say.

"Do you know," Dougal said, "up at the police station they are excavating an underground tunnel which starts in the station yard and runs all the way to Nunhead. You should ponder sometimes about underground tunnels. Did you know Boadicea was broken and defeated on the Rye? She was a great beefy soldier. I think you should take Mr. Druce's advice and study my manner, Mr. Weedin. I could give you lessons at ten and six an hour."

Mr. Weedin rose to hit him, but since the walls of his office were made mostly of glass, he was prevented in the act by an overwhelming sense of being looked at from all sides.

Dougal sat in Miss Frierne's panelled hall on Saturday morning and telephoned to the Flaxman number on the little slip of paper which Merle Coverdale had handed to him the previous day.

"Miss Cheeseman, please," said Dougal.

"She isn't in," said the voice from across the water. "Who shall I say it was?"

"Mr. Dougal-Douglas," Dougal said, "spelled with a hyphen. Tell Miss Cheeseman I'll be at home all morning."

He next rang Jinny.

"Hallo, are you better?" he said.

"I've got soup on the stove. I'll ring you back."

Miss Frierne was ironing in the kitchen. She said to Dougal, "Humphrey is going to see to the roof this afternoon. It's creaking. It isn't a loose slate, it must be one of the beams loose in his cupboard."

"Funny thing," Dougal said, "it only creaks at night. It goes Creak-oop!" The dishes rattled in their rack as he leapt.

"It's the cold makes it creak, I daresay," she said.

The telephone rang. Dougal rushed out to the hall. It was not Jinny, however.

"Doug dear," said Miss Maria Cheeseman from across the river.

"Oh, it's you, Cheese."

"We really must get down to things," Miss Cheeseman said. "All this about my childhood in Peckham, it's all wrong, it was Streatham."

"There's the law of libel to be considered," Dougal said. "A lot of your early associates in Streatham are still alive. If you want to write the true story of your life you can't place it in Streatham."

"But Doug dear," she said, "that bit where you make me say I played with Harold Lloyd and Ford Sterling at the Golden Domes in Camberwell, it isn't true, dear. I *was* in a show with Fatty Arbuckle but it was South Shields."

"I thought it was a work of art you wanted to write," Dougal said, "now was that not so? If you only want to write a straight autobiography you should have got a straight ghost. I'm crooked."

"Well, Doug dear, I don't think this story about me and the Gordon Highlander is quite nice, do you? I mean to say, it isn't true. Of course it's funny about the kilt, but it's a little embarrassing—"

"Well, write your own autobiography," Dougal said.

"Oh, Doug dear, do come over to tea."

"No, you've hurt my feelings."

"Doug dear, I'm thrilled with my book. I'm sure it's going to be marvelous. I can't say I'm quite happy about all of chapter three but—"

"What's wrong with chapter three?"

"Well, it's only that last bit you wrote, it isn't *me*."

"I'll see you at four o'clock," he said, "but understand, Cheese, I don't like crossing the water when I'm in the middle of a work of art. I'm giving all my time to it."

Dougal said to Humphrey, "I was over the other side of the river on business this afternoon, and while I was over that way I called in to see my girl."

"Oh, you got a girl over there?"

"Used to have. She's got engaged to somebody else."

"Women have no moral sense," Humphrey said. "You see it in the Unions. They vote one way then go and act another way."

"She was nice, Jinny," Dougal said, "but she was too delicate in health. Do you believe in the Devil?"

"No."

"Do you know anyone that believes in the Devil?"

"I think some of those Irish—"

"Feel my head," Dougal said.

"What?"

"Feel these little bumps up here." Dougal guided Humphrey's hand among his curls at each side. "I had it done by plastic surgeon," Dougal said.

"What?"

"He did an operation and took away the two horns. They had to shave my head in the nursing home before the operation. It took a long time for my hair to grow again."

Humphrey smiled and felt again among Dougal's curls.

"A couple of cysts," he said. "I've got one myself at the back of my head. Feel it."

Dougal touched the bump like a connoisseur.

"You supposed to be the Devil, then?" Humphrey asked.

"No, oh, no, I'm only supposed to be one of the wicked spirits that wander through the world for the ruin of souls. Have you mended those beams in the roof yet, that go Creak-oop?"

"I have," Humphrey said. "Dixie refused to come anymore."

6

"What strikes me as remarkable," Dougal said, "is how he manages to get in so much outside his school hours."

Nelly Mahone nodded, trod out her cigarette-end, and looked at the packet of cigarettes which Dougal had placed on the table.

"Help yourself," Dougal said, and he lit the cigarette for her.

"Ta," said Nelly. She looked round her room. "It's all *clean* dirt," she said.

"You would think," Dougal said, "his parents would have some control over him."

Nelly inhaled gratefully. "Up the Elephant, that's where they all go. What was name?"

"Leslie Crewe. Thirteen years of age. The father's manager of Beverly Hills Outfitters at Brixton."

"Where they live?"

"Twelve Rye Grove."

Nelly nodded. "How much you paid him?"

"A pound the first time, thirty bob the second time. But now he's asking five quid a week flat."

Nelly whispered, "Then there's a gang behind him, surely. Can't you give up one of the jobs for a month or two?"

"I don't see why I should," Dougal said, "just to please a thirteen-year-old blackmailer."

Nelly made signs with her hands and moved her mouth soundlessly, and swung her eyes to the wall between her room and the next, to show that the walls had ears.

"A thirteen-year-old blackmailer," Dougal said, more softly. But Nelly did not like the word blackmailer at all; she placed her old fish-smelling hand over Dougal's mouth, and whispered in his ear—her gray long hair falling against his nose—"A lousy fellow next door," she said. "A slob that wouldn't do a day's work if you paid him gold. So guard your mouth." She released Dougal and started to draw the curtains.

"And here's me," Dougal said, "willing to do three, four, five men's jobs, and I get blackmailed on grounds of false pretenses."

She ran with her long low dipping strides to his side and gave him a hard poke in the back. She returned to her window, which was as opaque as sackcloth and not really distinguishable from the curtain she pulled across it. On the floorboards were a few strips of very worn-out matting of a similar color. The bed in the corner was much of the same hue, lumpy and lopsided. "But I'm charmed to see you, all the same," Nelly said for the third time, "and will you have a cup of tea?"

Dougal said, no thanks, for the third time.

Nelly scratched her head, and raising her voice, declared, "Praise be to God, who rewards those who meditate the truths he has proposed for their intelligence."

"It seems to me," Dougal said, "that my course in life has much support from the Scriptures."

"Never," Nelly said, shaking her thin body out of its ecstasy and taking a cigarette out of Dougal's packet.

"Consider the story of Moses in the bullrushes. That was a crafty trick. The mother got her baby back and all expenses paid into the bargain. And consider the parable of the Unjust Steward. Do you know the parable of—"

"Stop," Nelly said, with her hand on her old blouse. "I get that excited by Holy Scripture I'm afraid to get my old lung trouble back."

"Were you born in Peckham?" Dougal said.

"No, Galway. I don't remember it though. I was a girl in Peckham."

"Where did you work?"

"Shoe factory I started life. Will you have a cup of tea?"

Dougal took out ten shillings.

"It's not enough," Nelly said.

Dougal made it a pound.

"If I got to follow them fellows round between here and the Elephant you just think of the fares alone," Nelly said. "I'll need more than that to go along with."

"Two quid, then," Dougal said. "And more next week."

"All right," she said.

"Otherwise it's going to be cheaper to pay Leslie."

"No it isn't," she said. "They go on and on wanting more and more. I hope you'll remember me nice if I get some way to stop their gobs."

"Ten quid," said Dougal.

"All right," she said. "But suppose one of your bosses finds out in the meantime? After all, rival firms is like to get nasty."

"Tell me," Dougal said, "how old are you?"

"I should say I was sixty-four. Have a cup of tea." She looked round the room. "It's all clean dirt."

"Tell me," Dougal said, "what it was like to work in the shoe factory."

She told him all of her life in the shoe factory till it was time for her to go out on her rounds proclaiming. Dougal followed her down the sour dark winding stairs of Lightbody Buildings, and they parted company in the passage, he going out before her.

"Good night, Nelly."

"Good night, Mr. Doubtless."

"Where's Mr. Douglas?" said Mr. Weedin.

"Haven't seen him for a week," Merle Coverdale replied. "Would you like me to ring him up at home and see if he's all right?"

"Yes, do that," Mr. Weedin said. "No, don't. Yes, I don't see why not. No, perhaps, though, we'd—"

Merle Coverdale stood tapping her pencil on her notebook, watching Mr. Weedin's hands shuffling among the papers on his desk.

"I'd better ask Mr. Druce," Mr. Weedin said. "He probably knows where Mr. Douglas is."

"He doesn't," Merle said.

"Doesn't he?"

"No, he doesn't."

"Wait till tomorrow. See if he comes in tomorrow."

"Are you feeling all right, Mr. Weedin?"

"Who? Me? I'm all right."

Merle went in to Mr. Druce. "Dougal hasn't been near the place for a week."

"Leave him alone. The boy's doing good work."

She returned to Mr. Weedin and stood in his open door with an exaggerated simper. "We are to leave him alone. The boy's doing good work."

"Come in and shut the door," said Mr. Weedin.

She shut the door and approached his desk.

"I'm not much of a believer," Mr. Weedin said, quivering his hands across the papers before him. "But there's something Mr. Douglas told me that's on my mind." He craned upward to look through the glass panels on all sides of his room.

"They're all out at tea-break," Merle said.

Mr. Weedin dropped his head on his hands. "It may

surprise you," he said, "coming from me. But it's my belief that Dougal Douglas is a diabolical agent, if not in fact the Devil."

"Mr. Weedin," said Miss Coverdale.

"Yes, I know what you're thinking. Yes, yes, you're thinking I'm going wrong up here." He pointed to his right temple and screwed it with his finger. "Do you know," he said, "that Douglas himself showed me bumps on his head where he had horns removed by plastic surgery?"

"Don't get excited, Mr. Weedin. Don't shout. The girls are coming up from the canteen."

"I felt those bumps with these very hands. Have you looked, have you ever properly looked at his eyes? That shoulder—"

"Keep calm, Mr. Weedin, you aren't getting yourself anywhere, you know."

Mr. Weedin pointed with a shaking arm in the direction of the managing director's office. "He's bewitched," he said.

Merle took tiny steps backward and got herself out of the door. She went in to Mr. Druce again.

"Mr. Weedin will be wanting a holiday," she said.

Mr. Druce lifted his paper-knife, toyed with it in his hand, pointed it at Merle, and put it down. "What did you say?" he said.

Drover Willis's was humming with work when Dougal reported on Friday morning to the managing director.

"During my first week," Dougal told Mr. Willis, "I have been observing the morals of Peckham. It seemed to me that the moral element lay at the root of all industrial discontents which lead to absenteeism and the slackness at work which you described to me."

Mr. Willis looked with his blue eyes at his rational

compatriot sitting before him with a shiny brief-case on his lap.

Mr. Willis said at last, "That would seem to be the correct approach, Mr. Dougal."

Dougal sat easily in his chair and continued his speech with half-closed, detached and scholarly eyes.

"There are four types of morality observable in Peckham," he said. "One, emotional. Two, functional. Three, puritanical. Four, Christian."

Mr. Willis opened the lid of a silver cigarette-box and passed it over to Dougal.

"No, thank you," Dougal said. "Take the first category, Emotional. Here, for example, it is considered immoral for a man to live with a wife who no longer appeals to him. Take the second, Functional, in which the principal factor is class solidarity such as, in some periods and places, has also existed amongst the aristocracy, and of which the main manifestation these days is the trade union movement. Three, Puritanical, of which there are several modern variants, monetary advancement being the most prevalent gauge of the moral life in this category. Four, Traditional, which accounts for about one percent of the Peckham population, and which in its simplest form is Christian. All moral categories are of course intermingled. Sometimes all are to be found in the beliefs and behavior of one individual."

"Where does this get us?"

"I can't say," Dougal said. "It is only a preliminary analysis."

"Please embody all this in a report for us, Mr. Dougal."

Dougal opened his brief-case and took out two sheets of paper. "I have elaborated on the question here. I have included case histories."

Mr. Willis smiled with one side of his mouth and

said, "Which of these four moral codes would you say was most attractive, Mr. Dougal?"

"Attractive?" Dougal said with a trace of disapproval.

"Attractive to us. Useful, I mean, useful."

Dougal pondered seriously until Mr. Willis's little smile was forced, for dignity's sake, to fade. Then, "I could not decide until I had further studied the question."

"We'll expect another report next week?"

"No, I'll need a month," Dougal stated. "A month to work on my own. I can't come in here again for a month if you wish me to continue research on this line of industrial psychology."

"You must see round the factory," said Mr. Willis. "Peckham is a big place. We're concerned with our own works first of all."

"I've arranged to be shown round this afternoon," Dougal said. "And at the end of a month I hope to spend some time with the workers in the recreation halls and canteens."

Mr. Willis looked silently at Dougal who then permitted himself a slight display of enthusiasm. He leaned forward.

"Have you observed, Mr. Willis, the frequency with which your employees use the word 'immoral'? Have you noticed how equally often they use the word 'ignorant'? These words are significant," Dougal said, "psychologically and sociologically."

Mr. Willis smiled, as far as he was able, into Dougal's face. "Take a month and see what you can do," he said. "But bring us a good plan of action at the end of it. Drover, my partner, is anxious about absenteeism. We want some moral line that will be both commendable by us and acceptable to our staff. You've got some sound ideas, I can see that. And method. I like method."

Dougal nodded and took his long serious face out of the room.

Miss Frierne said, "That boy Leslie Crewe has been here. He was looking for you. Wants to go your errands and make a bob like a good kid. Perhaps his mother's a bit short."

"Anyone with him?"

"No. He came to the back door this time."

"Oh," Dougal said, "did you get rid of him quickly?"

"Well, he wouldn't go for a long time. He kept saying when would Mr. Douglas be home, and could he do anything for you. He was very polite, I will say that. Then he asked the time and then he said his Dad used to live up this road in number eight. So I took him in the kitchen. I thought, well, he's only a boy, and gave him a doughnut. He said his sister was looking forward to marrying Humphrey in September. He said she saves all her wages and the father in America dresses her. He said—"

"He must have kept you talking a long time," Dougal said.

"Oh, I didn't mind. It was a nice break in the afternoon. A nice lad, he is. He goes out Sundays with the Rover Scouts. I'd just that minute come in and I was feeling a bit upset because of something that happened in the street, so—"

"Did he ask if he could go up and wait in my room?"

"No, not this time. I wouldn't have let him in your room, especially after you said nobody was to be let in there. Don't you worry about your room. Nobody wants to go into your room, I'm sure."

Dougal said, "You are too innocent for this wicked world."

"Innocent I always was," Miss Frierne said, "and that was why I was so taken aback that day by the

Gordon Highlander up on One Tree Hill. Have a cup of tea."

"Thanks," Dougal said. "I'll just pop upstairs a minute first."

His room had, of course, been disturbed. He unlocked a drawer in his dressing-table and found that two notebooks were missing. His portable typewriter had been opened and clumsily shut. Ten five-pound notes were, however, untouched in another drawer by the person who had climbed to his room while Leslie had engaged Miss Frierne in talk.

He came down to the kitchen where Miss Frierne sighed into her tea.

"Next time that Leslie comes round to the back door have a look, will you, to see who he's left at the front door. His father's worried about his companions after school hours, I happen to know."

"He only wanted to know if you had any errands to run. I daresay to help his mother, like a good kid. I told him I thought you're short of bacon for your breakfast. He'll be back. There's no harm in that boy, I know it by instinct, and instinct always tells. Like what happened to me in the street to-day." She sipped her tea, and was silent.

Dougal sipped his. "Go on," he said, "you're dying to tell me what happened."

"As true as God is my judge," she said, "I saw my brother up at Camberwell Green that left home in nineteen-nineteen. We never heard a word from him all those years. He was coming out of Lyons."

"Didn't you go and speak to him?"

"No," she said, "I didn't. He was very shabby, he looked awful. Something stopped me. It was an instinct. I couldn't do it. He saw me, too."

She took a handkerchief out of her sleeve and patted beneath her glasses.

"You should have gone up to him," Dougal said.

"You should have said, 'Are you . . .'—what was his name?"

"Harold," she said.

"You should have said, 'Are you Harold?', that's what you ought to have done. Instead of which you didn't. You came back here and gave a doughnut to that rotten little Leslie."

"Don't you point your finger at me, Dougal. Nobody does that in my house. You can find other accommodation *if* you like, any *time* you like and when you like."

Dougal got up and shuffled round the kitchen with a slouch and an old ill look. "Is that what your old brother looked like?" he said.

She laughed in high-pitched ripples.

Dougal thrust his hands into his pockets and looked miserable at his toes.

She started to cry all over her spectacles.

"Perhaps it wasn't your brother at all," Dougal said.

"That's what I'm wondering, son."

"Just feel my head," Dougal said, "these two small bumps here."

"There are four types of morality in Peckham," Dougal said to Mr. Druce. "The first category is—"

"Dougal," he said, "are you doing anything tonight?"

"Well, I usually prepare my notes. You realize, don't you, that Oliver Goldsmith taught in a school in Peckham? He used to commit absenteeism and spent a lot of his time in a coffee-house at the Temple instead of in Peckham. I wonder why?"

"I need your advice," Mr. Druce said. "There's a place in Soho—"

"I don't like crossing the river," Dougal said, "not without my broomstick."

Mr. Druce made double chins and looked lovingly at Dougal.

"There's a place in Soho—"

"I could spare a couple of hours," Dougal said. "I could see you up at Dulwich at the 'Dragon' at nine."

"Well, I was thinking of making an evening of it, Dougal; some dinner at this place in Soho—"

"Nine at the 'Dragon,' " Dougal said.

"Mrs. Druce knows a lot of people in Dulwich."

"All the better," Dougal said.

Dougal arrived at the "Dragon" at nine sharp. He drank gin and peppermint while he waited. At half-past nine two girls from Drover Willis's came in. Dougal joined them. Mr. Druce did not come. At ten o'clock they went on a bus to the "Rosemary Branch" in Southampton Way. Here, Dougal expounded the idea that everyone should take every second Monday morning off their work. When they came out of the pub, at eleven, Nelly Mahone crossed the street toward them.

"Praise be to the Lord," she cried, "whose providence in all things never fails."

"Hi, Nelly," said one of the girls as she passed.

Nelly raised up her voice and in the same tone proclaimed, "Praise be to God who by sin is offended, Trevor Lomas, Collie Gould up the Elephant with young Leslie, and by penance appeased, the exaltation of the humble and the strength of the righteous."

"Ah, Nelly," Dougal said.

7

"Yes, Cheese?" Dougal said.

"Look, Doug, I think I can't have this story about the 'Dragon' at Dulwich, it's indecent. Besides, it isn't true. And I never went to Soho at that age. I never went out with any managing director—"

"It will help to sell the book," Dougal said. He breathed moistly on the oak panel of Miss Frierne's hall, and with his free hand drew a face on the misty surface where he had breathed.

"And Doug dear," said the voice from across the river, "how did you know I started life in a shoe factory? I mean to say, *I* didn't tell you that. How did you know?"

"I didn't know, Cheese," Dougal said.

"You must have known. You've got all the details right, except that it wasn't in Peckham, it was Streatham. It all came back to me as I read it. It's uncanny. You've been checking up on me, haven't you, Doug?"

"Aye," Dougal said. He breathed on the panel, wrote in a word, then rubbed it off.

"Doug, you mustn't do that. It makes me creepy to think that people can find out all about you," Miss Cheeseman said. "I mean, I don't want to put in about the shoe factory and all that. Besides, the period. It dates me."

"It only makes you sixty-eight, Cheese."

"Well, Doug, there must be a way of making me not even that. I want you to come over, Doug. I've been feeling off color."

"I've got a fatal flaw," Dougal said, "to the effect that I can't bear anyone off color. Moreover, Saturday's my day off and it's a beautiful summer day."

"Dear Doug, I promise to be well. Only come over. I'm *worried* about my book. It's rather . . . rather too . . ."

"Rambling," Dougal said.

"Yes, that's it."

"I'll see you at four," Dougal said.

At the back of Hollis's Hamburgers at Elephant and Castle was a room furnished with a fitted gray carpet, a red upholstered modern suite comprising a sofa and two cubic armchairs, a television receiver on a light wood stand, a low glass-topped coffee table, a table on which stood an electric portable gramophone and a tape recorder, a light wood bureau desk, a standard lamp and several ash-trays on stands. Two of the walls were papered with a wide gray stripe. The other two were covered with a pattern of gold stars on red. Fixed to the walls were a number of white brackets containing pots of indoor ivy. The curtains, which were striped red and white, were drawn. This cheerful interior was lit by a couple of red-shaded wall-lamps. In one chair sat Leslie Crewe, with his neck held rigidly and attentively. He was dressed in a navy-blue suit of normal cut, and a peach-colored tie, and looked older than thirteen. In another chair lolled Collie Gould who was eighteen and had been found unfit for National Service; Collie suffered from lung trouble for which he was constantly under treatment and was at present on probation for motor stealing. He wore a dark-gray draped jacket with narrow black trousers. Trevor Lomas, dressed in blue-gray, lay between them on the sofa. All smoked American cigarettes. All looked miserable, not as an expression of their feelings, but as if by an instinctive prearrangement, to convey a decision on all affairs whatsoever.

Trevor held in his hand one of the two thin exercise books he had stolen from Dougal's drawer. The other lay on the carpet beside him.

"Listen to this," Trevor said. "It's called 'Phrases suitable for Cheese.' "

"Suitable for what?" said Collie.

"Cheese, it says. Code word, obvious. Listen to this what you make of it. There's a list.

"I thrilled to his touch
"I was too young at the time to understand why my mother was crying
"As he entered the room a shudder went through my frame
"In that moment of silent communion we renewed our shattered faith
"She was to play a vital role in my life
"Memory had not played me false
"He was always an incurable romantic
"I became the proud owner of a bicycle
"He spoke to me in desiccated tones
"Autumn again. Autumn. The burning of leaves in the park
"He spelled disaster to me
"I revelled in my first tragic part
"I had no eyes for any other man
"We were living a lie
"She proved a mine of information
"Once more fate intervened
"Munificence was his middle name
"I felt a grim satisfaction
"They were poles apart
"I dropped into a fitful doze."

"Read us it again, Trev," Leslie said. "It sounds like English Dictation. Perhaps he's a teacher as well."

Trevor ignored him. He tapped the notebook and addressed Collie.

"Code," he said. "It's worth lolly."

An intensified expression of misery on Collie's face expressed his agreement.

"In with a gang, he is. It's bigger than I thought. Question now, to find out what his racket is."

"Sex," Leslie said.

"You don't say so?" Trevor said. "Well, that's helpful, son. But we happen to have guessed all that. Question is, what game of sex? Question is, national or international?"

Collie blew out his smoke as if it were slow poison. "Got to work back from a clue," he said in his sick voice. "Autumn's a clue. Wasn't there something about autumn?"

"How dumb can you get?" Trevor inquired through his nose. "It's a code. Autumn means something else. Everything means something."

He dropped the notebook and painfully picked up the other. He read:

"Peckham. Modes of communication.

"Actions more effective than words. Enact everything. Depict.

"Morality. Functional. Emotional. Puritanical. Classical.

"Nelly Mahone. Lightbody Buildings.

"Tunnel. Meeting-house Lane Excavations police station yard. Order of St. Bridget. Nuns decamped in the night."

Trevor turned the pages.

[87]

Entry Parish Register 1658. May 5.

Rose, wife of Wm. Hathaway buried Aged 103, who boare a sonn at the age of 63.

Trevor said, "Definitely a code. Look how he spells 'son.' And this about bearing at the age of sixty-three."

Collie and Leslie came over to see the book.

"There's a clue here," Collie said, "that we could follow up."

"No," said Trevor, "you don't say so? Come on, kids, we got to look up Nelly Mahone."

"If we're going to have a row," Mavis said, "turn on the wireless loud."

"We're not going to have a row," said her husband, Arthur Crewe, in a voice trembling with patience. "I only ask a plain question, what you mean you can't ask him where he's going when he goes out?"

Mavis switched on the wireless to a roar. Then she herself shouted above it.

"If you want to know where he goes, ask him yourself."

"If you can't ask him how can I ask him?" Arthur said in competition with the revue on the wireless.

"What's it matter where he goes? You can't keep running about after him like he was a baby. He's thirteen now."

"You ought to a kept some control of him. Of course it's too late now—"

"Why didn't you keep some control—"

"How can I be at work and control the kids same time? If you was—"

"There's no need to swear," Mavis said.

"I didn't swear. But I bloody well will, and there's no need to shout." He turned off the wireless and silence occurred, bringing a definite aural sensation.

"Turn on that wireless. If we're going to have a row I'm not letting the neighbors get to know," Mavis said.

"Leave it be," Arthur said, effortful with peace. "There's not going to be any row."

Dixie came downstairs. "What's all the row?" she said.

"Your step-dad's on about young Leslie. Expects me to ask him where he's going when he goes out. I say, why don't *he* ask if he wants to know. I haven't got eyes the back of my head, have I?"

"Sh-sh-sh. Don't raise your voice," Arthur said.

"He's afraid to say a word to Leslie," Dixie said.

"That's just about it," said her mother.

"Who's afraid?" Arthur shouted.

"You are," Mavis shouted.

"I'm not afraid. You're afraid. . . ."

"Keep time," said Trevor. "All keep in time. It's psychological."

And so they all three trod in time up the stone stairs of Lightbody Buildings. Twice, a door opened on a landing, a head looked out, and the door shut quickly again. Trevor and his followers stamped louder as they approached Nelly Mahone's. Trevor beat like a policeman thrice on her door, and placed his ear to the crack.

There was a shuffling sound, a light switch clicked, then silence.

Trevor beat again.

"Who is it?" Nelly said from immediately on the other side of the door.

"Police agents," Trevor said.

The light switch clicked again, and Nelly opened the door a fragment.

Trevor pushed it wide open and walked in, followed by Collie and Leslie.

Leslie said, "I'm not stopping in this dirty hole," and made to leave.

[89]

Trevor caught him by the coat and worked him to a standstill.

"It's all clean dirt," Nelly said.

"Sit over there," Trevor said to Nelly, pointing to a chair beside the table. She did so.

He sat himself on the edge of the table and pointed to the edge of the bed for Leslie and the lopsided arm-chair for Collie.

"We come to talk business," Trevor said, "concerning a Mr. Dougal Douglas."

"Never heard of him," Nelly said.

"No?" Trevor said, folding his arms.

"Supposed to be police agents, are you? Well, you can be moving off if you don't want trouble. There's a gentleman asleep next door. I only got to raise me voice and—"

Collie and Leslie looked at the wall toward which Nelly pointed.

"Nark it," Trevor said. "He's gone to football this afternoon. Now, about Mr. Dougal Douglas—"

"Never heard of him," Nelly said.

Trevor leaned forward slightly toward her and, taking a lock of her long hair in his hand, twitched it sharply.

"Help! Murder! Police!" Nelly said.

Trevor put his big hand over her mouth and spoke to her.

"Listen, Nelly, for your own good. We got money for you."

Nelly struggled, her yellow eyeballs were big.

"I get my boys to rough you up if you won't listen, Nelly. Won't we, boys?"

"That's right," Collie said.

"Won't we, boys?" Trevor said, looking at Leslie.

"Sure," said Leslie.

Trevor removed his hand, now wet, from Nelly's mouth, and wiped it on the side of his trousers. He took a large wallet from his pocket, and flicked through a pile of bank notes.

"He's at Miss Frierne's up the Rye," Nelly said.

Trevor laid his wallet on the table and folding his arms, looked hard at Nelly.

"He got a job at Meadows Meade," Nelly said.

Trevor waited.

"He got another job at Drover Willis's under different name. No harm in him, son."

Trevor waited.

"That's all, son," Nelly said.

"What's cheese?" Trevor said.

"What's what?"

Trevor pulled her hair, so that she toppled toward him from her chair.

"I'll find out more. I only seen him once," Nelly said.

"What he want with you?"

"Huh?"

"You heard me."

Nelly looked at the two others, then back at Trevor.

"The boys is under age," she remarked, and her eyes flicked a little to reveal that her brain was working.

"I ask you a question," Trevor said. "What Mr. Dougal Douglas come to you for?"

"About the girl," she said.

"What girl?"

"He's after Beauty," she said. "He want me to find out where she live and that. You better go and see what he's up to. Probable he's with her now."

"Who's his gang?" Trevor inquired, reaching for Nelly's hair.

She jumped away from him. Leslie's nerve gave way and he ran to Nelly and hit her on the face.

"Murder!" Nelly screamed.

Trevor put his hand over her mouth, and signalled

with his eyes to Collie, who went to the door, opened it a little way, listened, then shut it again. Collie then struck Leslie, who backed onto the bed.

Trevor, with his big hand on Nelly's mouth, whispered softly in her ear,

"Who's his gang, Nelly? What's the code key? Ten quid to you, Nelly."

She squirmed and he took his moist hand from her mouth. "Who's his gang?"

"He goes with Miss Coverdale sometimes. He goes with that fair-haired lady controller that's gone to Drover Willis's. That's all I know of his company."

"Who are the fellows?"

"I'll find out," she said, "I'll find out, son. Have a heart."

"Who's Rose Hathaway?"

"Never heard of her."

Trevor took Dougal's rolled-up exercise book from an inside pocket and spreading it out at the page read out the bit about that Rose Hathaway who was buried at a hundred and three. "That mean anything to you?" Trevor said.

"It sounds all wrong. I'll ask him."

"You won't. You'll find out your own way. Not a word we been here, get that?"

"It's only his larks. He's off his nut, son."

"Did he by any chance bring Humphrey Place here with him?"

"Who?"

Trevor twisted her arm.

"Humphrey Place. Goes with Dixie Morse."

"No, never seen him but once at the 'Grapes.' "

"You'll be seeing *us* again," Trevor said.

He went down the dark stone stairs followed by Leslie and Collie.

* * *

"Killing herself," Merle said, "that's what she is, for money. Then she comes in to the pool dropping tired next day, not fit for the job. I said to her, 'Dixie,' I said, 'what time did you go to bed last night?' 'I consider that a personal question, Miss Coverdale,' she says. 'Oh,' I says, 'well, if it isn't a personal question will you kindly type these two reports over again? There's five mistakes on one and six on the other.' 'Oh!' she said, 'what mistakes?' Because she won't own up to her mistakes till you put them under her nose. I said, 'These mistakes as marked.' She said 'Oh!' I said, 'You've been doing nothing but yawn yawn yawn all week.' Well, at tea-break when Dixie was out Connie says to me, 'Miss Coverdale, it's Dixie's evening job making her tired.' 'Evening job?' I said. She said, 'Yes, she's an usherette at the Regal from six-thirty to ten-thirty, makes extra for her wedding savings.' 'Well,' I said, 'no wonder she can't do her job here!'"

Dougal flashed an invisible cinema-torch on to the sprightly summer turf of the Rye. "Mind the step, Madam. Three-and-sixes on the right."

Merle began to laugh from her chest. Suddenly she sat down on the Rye and began to cry. "God!" she said. "Dougal, I've had a rotten life."

"And it isn't over yet," Dougal said, sitting down beside her at a little distance. "There might be worse ahead."

"First my parents," she said. "Too possessive. They're full of themselves. They don't think anything of me myself. They like to be able to say 'Merle's head of the pool at Meadows Meade,' but that's about all there is to it. I broke away and of course like a fool took up with Mr. Druce. Now I can't get away from him, somehow. You've unsettled me, Dougal, since you came to Peckham. I shall have a nervous breakdown, I can see it coming."

"If you do," Dougal said, "I won't come near you. I can't bear sickness of any sort."

"Dougal," she said, "I was counting on you to help me to get away from Mr. Druce."

"Get another job," he said, "and refuse to see him any more. It's easy."

"Oh, everything's easy for you. You're free."

"Aren't you free?" Dougal said.

"Yes, as far as the law goes."

"Well, stop seeing Druce."

"After six years, going on seven, Dougal, I'm tied in a sort of way. And what sort of job would I get at thirty-eight?"

"You would have to come down," Dougal said.

"After being head of the pool," she said, "I couldn't. I've got to think of my pride. And there's the upkeep of my flat. Mr. Druce puts a bit toward it."

"People are looking at you crying," Dougal said, "and they think it's because of me."

"So it is in a way. I've had a rotten life."

"Goodness, look at that," Dougal said.

She looked upward to where he was pointing.

"What?" she said.

"Up there," Dougal said; "trees in the sky."

"What are you talking about? I don't see anything."

"Look properly," Dougal said, "up there. And don't look away because Mr. Druce is watching us from behind the pavilion."

She looked at Dougal.

"Keep looking up," he said, "at the trees with red tassels in the sky. Look, where I'm pointing."

Several people who were crossing the Rye stopped to look up at where Dougal was pointing. Dougal said to them, "A new idea. Did you see it in the papers? Planting trees and shrubs in the sky. Look there—it's a tip of a pine."

"I think I *do* see something," said a girl.

Most of the crowd moved skeptically away, still glancing upward now and then. Dougal brought Merle to her feet and drifted along with the others.

"Is he still there?" Merle said.

"Yes. He must be getting tired of going up and down in lifts."

"Oh, he only does that on Saturday mornings. He usually stays at home in the afternoons. He comes to me in the evenings. I've got a rotten life. Sometimes I think I'll swallow a bottle of aspirins."

"That doesn't work," Dougal said. "It only makes you ill. And the very thought of illness is abhorrent to me."

"He's keen on you," Merle said.

"I know he is, but *he* doesn't."

"He must do if he's keen—"

"Not at all. I'm his first waking experience of an attractive man."

"You fancy yourself."

"No, Mr. Druce does that."

"With your crooked shoulder," she said, "you're not all that much cop."

"Advise Druce on those lines," he said.

"He doesn't take my advice any more."

"How long would you give him with the firm?"

"Well, since he's started to slip, I've debated that question a lot. The business is on the decline. It's a worry, I mean about my flat, if Mr. Druce loses his job."

"I'd give him three months," Dougal said.

Merle started to cry again, walking towards the streets with Dougal. "Is he still there?" she said. Dougal did a dancer's pirouette, round and round, and stopped once more by Merle's side.

"He's walking away in the other direction."

"Oh, I wonder where he's going?"

"Home to Dulwich, I expect."

"It's immoral," Merle said, "the way he goes back to that woman in that house. They never say a word to each other."

"Stop girning. You look awful with your red eyes. It detracts from the Okapi look. But all the same, what a long neck you've got!"

She put her hand up to her throat and moved it up her long neck. "Mr. Druce squeezed it tight the other day," she said, "for fun, but I got a fright."

"It looks like a maniac's delight, your neck," Dougal said.

"Well, you've not got much of one, with your shoulder up round your ear."

"A short neck denotes a good mind," Dougal said. "You see, the messages go quicker to the brain because they've shorter to go." He bent and touched his toes. "Suppose the message starts down here. Well, it comes up here—"

"Watch out, people are looking."

They were in the middle of Rye Lane, flowing with shopping women and prams. A pram bumped into Dougal as he stood upright, causing him to barge forward into two women who stood talking. Dougal embraced them with wide arms. "Darlings, watch where you're going," he said. They beamed at each other and at him.

"Charming, aren't you?" Merle said. "There's a man leaning out of that car parked outside Higgins and Jones, seems to be watching you."

Dougal looked across the road. "Mr. Willis is watching me," he said. "Come and meet Mr. Willis." He took her arm to cross the road.

"I'm not dressed for an introduction," Merle said.

"You are only an object of human research," Dougal said, guiding her obliquely through the traffic toward Mr. Willis.

"I'm just waiting for my wife. She's shopping in

there," Mr. Willis explained. Now that Dougal had approached him he seemed rather embarrassed. "I wasn't sure it was you, Mr. Dougal," he explained. "I was just looking to see. A bit short-sighted."

"Miss Merle Coverdale, one of my unofficial helpers," Dougal said uppishly. "Interesting," he said, "to see what Peckham does on its Saturday afternoons."

"Yes, quite." Mr. Willis pinkly took Merle's hand and glanced toward the shop door.

Dougal gave a reserved nod and, as dismissing Mr. Willis from his thoughts, led Merle away.

"Why did he call you Mr. Dougal?" Merle said.

"Because he's my social inferior. Formerly a footman in our family."

"What's he now?"

"One of my secret agents."

"You'd send me mad if I let you. Look what you've done to Weedin. You're driving Mr. Druce up the wall."

"I have powers of exorcism," Dougal said, "that's all."

"What's that?"

"The ability to drive devils out of people."

"I thought you said you were a devil yourself."

"The two states are not incompatible. Come to the police station."

"Where are we going, Dougal?"

"The police station. I want to see the excavation."

He took her into the station yard where he had already made himself known as an interested archaeologist. By the coal-heap was a wooden construction above a cavity already some feet deep. Work had stopped for the week-end. They peered inside.

"The tunnel leads up to Nunhead," Dougal said, "the nuns used to use it. They packed up one night over a hundred years ago, and did a flit, and left a lot of debts behind them."

A policeman came up to them with quiet steps and, pointing to the coal-heap, said, "The penitential cell stood in that corner. Afternoon, sir."

"Goodness, you gave me a fright," Merle said.

"There's bodies of nuns down there, miss," the policeman said.

Merle had gone home to await Mr. Druce. Dougal walked up to Costa's Café in the cool of the evening. Eight people were inside, among them Humphrey and Dixie, seated at a separate table eating the remains of sausage and egg. Humphrey kicked out a chair at their table for Dougal to sit down upon. Dixie touched the corners of her mouth with a paper napkin, and carefully picking up her knife and fork, continued eating, turning her head a little obliquely to receive each small mouthful. Humphrey had just finished. He set down his knife and fork on the plate and pushed the plate away. He rubbed the palms of his hands together twice and said to Dougal,

"How's life?"

"It exists," Dougal said, and looked about him.

"You had a distinguished visitor this afternoon. But you'd just gone out. The old lady was out and I answered to him. He wouldn't leave his name. But of course I knew it. Mr. Druce of Meadows Meade. Dixie pointed him out to me, once, didn't you, Dixie?"

"Yes," Dixie said.

"He followed me all over the Rye, so greatly did Mr. Druce wish to see me," Dougal said.

"If I was you," Humphrey said, "I'd keep to normal working hours. Then he wouldn't have any call on you Saturday afternoons—would he, Dixie?"

"I suppose not," Dixie said.

"Coffee for three," Dougal said to the waiter.

"You had another visitor, about four o'clock,"

Humphrey said. "I'll give you a clue. She had a pot of flowers and a big parcel."

"Elaine," Dougal said.

The waiter brought three cups of coffee, one in his right hand and two—one resting on the other—in his left. These he placed carefully on the table. Dixie's slopped over in her saucer. She looked at the saucer.

"Swap with me," Humphrey said.

"Have mine," Dougal said.

She allowed Humphrey to exchange his saucer with hers. He tipped the contents of the saucer into his coffee, sipped it, and set it down.

"Sugar," he said.

Dougal passed the sugar to Dixie.

She said, "Thank you." She took two lumps, dropped them in her coffee, and stirred it, watching it intently.

Humphrey put three lumps in his coffee, stirred it rapidly, tasted it. He pushed the sugar bowl over to Dougal, who took a lump and put it in his mouth.

"I let her go up to your room," Humphrey said. "She said she wanted to put in some personal touches. There was the pot of flowers and some cretonne cushions. The old lady was out. I thought it nice of Elaine to do that—wasn't it nice, Dixie?"

"Wasn't what nice?"

"Elaine coming to introduce feminine touches in Dougal's room."

"I suppose so."

"Feeling all right?" Humphrey said to her.

"I suppose so."

"Do you want to go on somewhere else or do you want to stay here?"

"Anything you like."

"Have a cake."

"No, thank you."

"Why does your brother go hungry?" Dougal said to her.

"Whose brother goes hungry?"

"Yours. Leslie."

"What you mean, goes hungry?"

"He came round scrounging doughnuts off my landlady the other day," Dougal said.

Humphrey rubbed the palms of his hands together and smiled at Dougal. "Oh, kids, you know what they're like."

"I won't stand for him saying anything against Leslie," Dixie said, looking round to see if anyone at the other tables was listening. "Our Leslie isn't a scrounger. It's a lie."

"It is not a lie," Dougal said.

"I'll speak to my step-dad," Dixie said.

"I should," Dougal said.

"What's a doughnut to a kid?" Humphrey said to them both. "Don't make something out of nothing. Don't *start*."

"Who started?" Dixie said.

"You did, a matter of fact," Humphrey said, "with your bad manners. You could hardly say hallo to Dougal when he came in."

"That's right, take his part," she said. "Well, I'm not staying here to be insulted."

She rose and picked up her bag. Dougal pulled her down to her chair again.

"Take your hand off me," she said, and rose.

Humphrey pulled her down again.

She remained seated, looking ahead into the far distance.

"There's Beauty just come in," Dougal said.

Dixie turned her head to see Beauty. Then she resumed her fixed gaze.

Dougal whistled in Beauty's direction.

"I shouldn't do that," Humphrey said.

"My God, he's supposed to be a professional man," Dixie said, "and he opens his mouth and whistles at a girl."

Dougal whistled again.

Beauty raised her eyebrows.

"You'll have Trevor Lomas in after us," Humphrey said. The waiter and Costa himself came and hovered round their table.

"Come on up to the 'Harbinger,'" Dougal said, "and we'll take Beauty with us."

"Now look. I quite *like* Trevor," Humphrey said.

"He's to be best man at our wedding," Dixie said. "He's got a good job with prospects and sticks in to it."

Dougal whistled. Then he called across two tables to Beauty, "Waiting for somebody?"

Beauty dropped her lashes. "Not in particular," she said.

"Coming up to the 'Harbinger'?"

"Don't mind."

Dixie said, "Well, *I* do. I'm fussy about my company."

"What she say?" Beauty said, jerking herself upright in support of the question.

"I said," said Dixie, "that I've got another appointment."

"Beauty and I will be getting along then," Dougal said. He went across to Beauty who was preparing to comb her hair.

Humphrey said, "After all, Dixie, we've got nothing else to do. It might look funny if we don't go with Dougal. If Trevor finds out he's been to a pub with his girl—"

"You're bored with me—*I* know," Dixie said. "My company isn't good enough for you as soon as Dougal comes on the scene."

"Such compliments as you pay me!" Dougal said across to her.

"I was not aware I was addressing you," Dixie said.

"All right, Dixie, we'll stop here," Humphrey said.

Dougal was holding up a small mirror while the girl combed her long copper-colored hair over the table.

Dixie's eyes then switched over to Dougal. She gave a long sigh. "I suppose we'd better go to the pub with them," she said, "or you'll say I spoiled your evening."

"No necessity," Beauty said as she put away her comb and patted her handbag.

"We might enjoy ourselves," Humphrey said.

Dixie got her things together rather excitedly. But she said, "Oh, it isn't my idea of a night out."

And so they followed Dougal and Beauty up Rye Lane to the "Harbinger." Beauty was halfway through the door of the saloon bar, but Dougal had stopped to look into the darkness of the Rye beyond the swimming baths, from which came the sound of a drunken woman approaching; and yet as it came nearer, it turned out not to be a drunken woman, but Nelly proclaiming.

Humphrey and Dixie had reached the pub door. "It's only Nelly," Humphrey said, and he pushed Dougal toward the doorway in which Beauty stood waiting.

"I like listening to Nelly," Dougal said, "for my human research."

"Oh, get inside for goodness' sake," Dixie said as Nelly appeared in the streetlight.

"Six things," Nelly declaimed, "there are which the Lord hateth, and the seventh his soul detesteth. Haughty eyes, a lying tongue, hands that shed innocent blood. See me in the morning. A heart that deviseth wicked plots, feet that are swift to run into mischief. Ten at Paley's yard. A deceitful witness that uttereth lies. Meeting-house Lane. And him that soweth discord among brethren.''

"Nelly's had a few," Humphrey said as they pushed into the bar. "She's a bit shaky on the pins tonight."

A bright spiky chandelier and a row of glittering crystal lamps set against a mirror behind the bar—though in fact these had been installed since the war—were designed to preserve in theory the pub's vintage fame in the old Camberwell Palace days. The chief barmaid had a tiny nose and a big chin; she was a middle-aged woman of twenty-five. The barman was small and lithe. He kept swinging to and fro on the balls of his feet.

Beauty wanted a martini. Dixie, at first under the impression that Humphrey was buying the round, asked for a ginger ale, but when she perceived that Dougal was to pay for the drinks, she said, "Gin and ginger ale." Humphrey and Dougal carried to a table the girls' drinks and their own half-pints of mild which glittered in knobbly-molded glass mugs like versions of the chandelier. Round the wall were hung signed photographs of old-time variety actors with such names, meaningless to most but oddly suggestive, as Flora Finch and Ford Sterling, who were generally assumed to be Edwardian stars. An upright piano placed flat against a wall caused Tony the pianist to see little of the life of the house, except when he turned round for a rest between numbers. Tony's face was not merely pale, but quite bloodless. He wore a navy-blue coat over a very white shirt, the shirt buttoned up to the neck with no tie. His half-pint mug, constantly replenished by the customers, stood on an invariable spot on the right-hand side of the piano-top. As he played, he swung his shoulders from side to side and bent over the piano occasionally to stress his notes. He might, from this back view, have been in an enthusiastic mood, but when he turned round it was obvious he was not. It was Tony's lot to play tunes of the nineteen-tens and -twenties, to the accompaniment of slightly jeering comments from the customers, and as he stooped over to execute "Charmain," Beauty said to him, "Groove in, Tony." He ignored this as he had ignored all remarks for the past nineteen months. "Go, man, go," someone suggested. "Leave him alone," the barmaid said. "You just show up your ignorance. He's a beautiful player. It's period stuff. He got to play it like that." Tony finished his number, took down his beer and turned his melancholy front to the company.

"Got any rock and cha-cha on your list, Tony?"

"Rev up to it, son. Groove in."

Tony turned, replaced his beer on the top of the piano, and rippled his hands over "Ramona."

"Go, man, go."

"Any more of that," said the barmaid, "and you go man go outside."

"Yes, that's what *I* say. Tony's the pops."

"Here's a pint, Tony. Cheer up, son, it may never happen."

At ten past nine Trevor Lomas entered the pub followed by Collie Gould. Trevor edged in to the bar and stood with his back to it, leaning on an elbow and surveying as it were the passing scene.

"Hallo, Trevor," Dixie said.

"Hi, Dixie," Trevor replied severely.

"Hi," Collie Gould said.

Beauty, who was on her fourth martini, bowed graciously, and had some difficulty in regaining her upright posture.

The barmaid said, "Are you ordering, sir?"

Trevor said over his shoulder, "Two pints bitter." He lit a cigarette and blew out the smoke very very slowly.

"Trev," Collie said in a low voice, "Trev, don't muck it up."

"I'm being patient," Trevor said through half-closed lips. "I'm being very very patient. But if—"

"Trev," Collie said, "Trev, think of the lolly. Them notebooks."

Trevor threw half-a-crown backward onto the counter.

"Manners," the barmaid said as she rang the till. She banged his change on the counter, where Trevor let it lie.

Dougal and Humphrey approached the bar with four empty glasses. "Ginger ale only," Dixie called after them, since it was Humphrey's turn.

"One martini. Two half milds. One *gin* and ginger ale," Humphrey said to the barmaid. And he invited Trevor to join them by pointing to their table with his ear.

Trevor did not move. Collie was watching Trevor.

Dougal got out some money.

"My turn," Humphrey said, fishing out his money.

Dougal picked half-a-crown from his money and, leaning his back against the bar, tossed it over his shoulder to the counter. He then lit a cigarette and blew out the smoke very slowly, pulling his face to a grave length and batting his eyelashes.

Beauty shouted, "Doug, you're a boy! Dig Doug! He'd got you, Trev. He does Trevor to a T." Tony was playing the St. Louis Blues.

"Trev," Collie said, "don't, Trev, don't."

Trevor raised his sparkling pint glass and smashed the top on the edge of the counter. In his hand remained the bottom half with six spikes of glass sticking up from it. He lunged it forward at Dougal's face. At the same swift moment Dougal leaned back, back, until the crown of his head touched the bar. The spikes of glass went full into one side of Humphrey's face which had been turned in profile. Dougal bent and caught Trevor's legs while another man pulled Trevor's collar until presently he lay pinned by a number of hands to the floor. Humphrey was being attended by another number of hands, and was taken to the back premises, the barmaid holding to his face a large thick towel which was becoming redder and redder.

The barman shouted above the din, "Outside, all."

Most of the people were leaving in any case lest they should be questioned. To those who lingered the barman shouted, "Outside, all, or I'll call the police."

Trevor found himself free to get to his feet and he left, followed by Collie and Beauty, who was seen to spit at Trevor before she clicked her way up Rye Lane.

Dixie remained behind with Dougal. She was saying to him, "It was meant for *you*. Dirty swine you were to duck."

"Outside or I call the police," the barman said, bouncing up and down on the balls of his feet.

"We were with the chap that's hurt," Dougal said, "and if we can't collect him *I'll* call the police."

"Follow me," said the barman.

Humphrey was holding his head over a bowl while cold water was being poured over his wounds by Tony, who seemed to take this as one of his boring evening duties.

"Goodness, you look terrible," Dougal said. "It must be my fatal flaw, but I doubt if I can bear to look."

"Dirty swine, he is," Dixie said, "letting another fellow have it instead of himself."

"Shut up, will you?" Humphrey seemed to say.

They got into Humphrey's car, speedily assisted by the barman. Dougal drove, first taking Dixie home. She said to him, "I could spit at you," and slammed the car door.

"Oh, shut up," Humphrey said, as well as he could.

Dougal next drove Humphrey to the outpatient department of St. George's Hospital. "Though it pains me to cross the river," Dougal said, "I think we'd better avoid the southern region for tonight."

He told a story about Humphrey's having tripped over a milk-bottle as he got out of his car, the milk-bottle having splintered and Humphrey fallen on his face among the splinters. Humphrey nodded agreement as the nurse dressed and plastered his wounds. Dougal gave Humphrey's name as Mr. Dougal-Douglas, care of Miss Cheeseman, 14 Chelsea Rise, S.W.3. Humphrey was told to return within a week. They then went to Miss Frierne's.

"And I won't even see her again till next Saturday night on account of her doing week-nights as an usherette at the Regal," Humphrey said to Dougal at a quarter to twelve that night. He sat up in bed in striped pajamas, talking as much as possible; but the strips of plaster on his cheek caused him to speak rather out of the opposite side of his mouth. "And she won't think of taking one day off of her holidays this year on account of the honeymoon in September. It's nothing but save, save, save. You'd think I wasn't earning good money the way she goes on. And result, she's losing her sex."

Dougal crouched over the gas-ring with a fork, pushing the bacon about in the frying-pan. He removed the bacon onto a plate, then broke two eggs into the pan.

"I wouldn't marry her," Dougal said, "if you paid me."

"My sister Elsie doesn't like her," Humphrey said out of the side of his mouth.

Dougal stood up and took the plate of bacon in his hand. He held this at some way from his body and looked at it, moving it slightly back and forth toward him, as if it were a book he was reading, and he short-sighted.

Dougal read from the book: "Wilt thou take this woman," he said with a deep ecclesiastical throb, "to be thai wedded waif?"

Then he put the plate aside and knelt; he was a sinister goggling bridegroom. "No," he declared to the ceiling, "I won't, quite frankly."

"Christ, don't make me laugh, it pulls the plaster."

Dougal dished out the eggs and bacon. He cut up the bacon small for Humphrey.

"You shouldn't have any scars if you're careful and get your face regularly dressed, they said."

Humphrey stroked his wounded cheek.

"Scars wouldn't worry me. Might worry Dixie."

"As a qualified refrigerator engineer and a union man you could have your pick of the girls."

"I know, but I want Dixie." He put the eggs and bacon slowly away into the side of his mouth.

The rain of a cold summer morning fell on Nelly Mahone as she sat on a heap of disused lorry tires in the yard of Paley's, scrap merchants of Meeting-house Lane. She had been waiting since ten past nine although she did not expect Dougal to arrive until ten o'clock. He came at five past ten, bobbing up and down under an umbrella.

"They come to see me Saturday," she said at once. "Trevor Lomas, Collie Gould, Leslie Crewe. They treated me bad."

"You've got wet," Dougal said. "Why didn't you take shelter?"

She looked round the yard. "Got to be careful where you go, son. Stand up in the open, they can only tell you to move on. But go inside a place, they can call the cops." Her nose thrust forward toward the police station at the corner of the lane.

Dougal looked round the yard for possible shelter. The bodies of two lorries, bashed in from bad accidents, stood lopsided in a corner. On a low wooden cradle stood a house-boat. "We'll go into the boat."

"Oh, I couldn't get up there."

Dougal kicked a wooden crate over and over till it stood beneath the door of the boat. He pulled the door-handle. Eventually it gave way. He climbed in, then out again, and took Nelly by the arm.

"Up you go, Nelly."

"What if the cops come?"

"I'm in with them," Dougal said.

"Jesus, that's not your game?"

"Up you go."

He heaved her up and settled in the boat beside her on a torn upholstered seat. Some sad cretonne curtains still drooped in the windows. Dougal drew them across the windows as far as was possible.

"I feel that ill," Nelly said.

"I'm not too keen on illness," Dougal said.

"Nor me. They come to ask after you," Nelly said. "They found out you was seeing me. They got your code. They want to know what's cheese. They want to know what's your code key, they offer me ten quid. They want to know who's your gang."

"I'm in with the cops, tell them."

"That I would never believe. They want to know who's Rose Hathaway. They'll be back again. I got to tell them something."

"Tell them I'm paid by the police to investigate certain irregularities in the industrial life of Peckham in the first place. See, Nelly? I mean crime at the top in the wee factories. And secondly—"

Her yellowish eyes and wet gray hair turned toward him in a startled way.

"If I thought you was a nark—"

"Investigator," Dougal said. "It all comes under human research. And secondly my job covers various departments of youthful terrorism. So you can just tell me, Nelly, what they did to you on Saturday afternoon.''

''Ah, they didn't do nothing out of the way.''

''You said they treated you roughly.''

''No, not so to get them in trouble.''

Dougal took out an envelope. ''Your ten pounds,'' he said.

''You can keep it,'' Nelly said. ''I'm going on my way.''

''Feel my head, Nelly.'' He guided her hand to the two small bumps among his curls.

''Cancer of the brain a-coming on,'' she said.

''Nelly, I had a pair of horns like a goat when I was born. I lost them in a fight at a later date.''

''Holy Mary, let me out of here. I don't know whether I'm coming or going with you.''

Dougal stood up and found that by standing astride in the middle of the boat he could make it rock. So he rocked it for a while and sang a sailor's song to Nelly.

Then he helped her to climb down from the boat, put up his umbrella and tried to catch up with her as she hurried out of the scrap yard. A policeman, coming out of the station, at the corner, nodded to Dougal.

''I'll be going into the station then, Nelly,'' Dougal said. ''To see my chums.''

She stared at him, then spat on the rainy pavement.

''And I don't mind,'' Dougal said, ''if you tell Trevor Lomas what I'm doing. You can tell him if he returns my notebooks to me there will be nothing further said. We policemen have got to keep our records and our secret codes, you realize.''

She moved sideways away from him, watching the traffic so that she could cross at the earliest moment.

''You and I,'' Dougal said, ''won't be molested from that quarter for a week or two if you give them the tip-off.''

He went into the station yard to see how the excavations were getting on. He discovered that the tunnel itself was now visible from the top of the shaft.

Dougal pointed out to his policemen friends the evidence of the Thames silt in the under-soil. "One time," he said, "the Thames was five miles wide, and it covered all Peckham."

So they understood, they said, from other archaeologists who were interested in the excavation.

"Hope I'm not troubling you if I pop in like this from time to time?" Dougal said.

"No, sir, you're welcome. We get people from the papers sometimes as well as students. Did you read of the finds?"

Toward evening a parcel was delivered at Miss Frierne's addressed to Dougal. It contained his notebooks.

"I hope to remain with you," Dougal said to Miss Frierne, "for at least two months. For I see no call upon me to remove from Peckham as yet."

"If I'm still alive . . ." Miss Frierne said. "I saw that man again this morning. I could swear it was my brother."

"You didn't speak to him?"

"No. Something stopped me." She began to cry.

"Who put the pot of indoor creeping ivy in my room?" Dougal said. "Was it my little dog-toothed blonde process-controller?"

"Yes, it was a scraggy little blonde. Looks as if she could do with a good feed. They all do."

Mr. Druce whispered, "I couldn't manage it the other night. Things were difficult."

"I sat at the 'Dragon' in Dulwich from nine till closing time," Dougal said, "and you didn't come."

"I couldn't get away. Mrs. Druce was on the watch. If you'd come to that place in Soho—"

Dougal consulted his pocket diary. He shut it and

put it away. "Next month it would have to be. This month my duties press." He rose and walked up and down Mr. Druce's office as with something on his mind.

"I called for you last Saturday," Mr. Druce said. "I thought you would care for a spin."

"So I understand," Dougal said absently. "I believe I was researching on Miss Coverdale that afternoon." Dougal smiled at Mr. Druce. "Interrogating her, you know."

"Oh, yes."

"Her devotion to you is quite remarkable," Dougal said. "She spoke of you continually."

"As a matter of interest, what did she say? Look, Dougal, you can't trust everyone—"

Dougal looked at his watch. "Goodness," he said, "the time. What I came to see you about—the question of my increase in salary."

"It's going through," Mr. Druce said. "I put it to the Board that, since Weedin's breakdown, a great deal of extra work falls on your shoulders."

Dougal massaged both his shoulders, first his high one, then his low one.

"Dougal," said Mr. Druce.

"Vincent," said Dougal, and departed.

8

Joyce Willis said, "Quite frankly, the first time Richard invited you to dinner I knew we'd found the answer. Richard didn't see it at first, quite frankly, but I think he's beginning to see it now."

She crossed the room, moving her long hips, and looked out of the bow window into the August evening. "Richard should be in any moment," she said. She touched her throat with her fine fingers. She put to rights a cushion in the window-seat.

Still standing, she lifted her glass, and sipped, and put it down on a low table. She crossed the room and sat on a chair upholstered in deep pink brocade.

"I feel I can really *talk* to you now," she said. "I feel we've known each other for years."

She said, "The Drovers *were* getting the upper hand. Richard was, well, quite frankly, being pushed into the position of subordinate partner.

"The nephew, Mark Bewlay—that's *her* nephew, of course—came to the firm two—was it two?—no, it was three years ago, imagine it, in October. And he was supposed to go through the factory from A to Z. Well, quite frankly he was sitting on the Board within six months. Then the son John came straight down from Oxford last year, and same thing again. The Board's recking with Drovers.

"One of Richard's great mistakes—I'm speaking to

you quite frankly," she said, "was insisting on our *living* in Peckham. Well, the house is all right—but I mean, the environment. There are simply no people in the place. Our friends always get lost finding the way here; they drive round for hours. And there are blacks at the other end of the Avenue, you know. I mean, it's so silly.

"Richard's a Scot, of course," she said, "and in a way that's why I think you understand his position. He's so scrupulously industrious and pathologically honest. And it's rather sweet in a way. Yes, I must say that. He simply doesn't see that the Drovers living in Sussex in a Georgian rectory gives them a big advantage. A big advantage. It's psychological."

She said, "Yes, Richard insists on living near the job, as he says. And quite frankly, I have to put up with a good deal of condescension from Queenie Drover, although she's sweet in a way. She knows of course that Richard's a bit old-fashioned and prides himself on being a *real merchant*, they both know, the Drovers. They know it only too well."

She filled both glasses with sherry, turning the good bones of her wrists and holding the glasses at the ends of her long fingers with their lacquered nails and the bright emerald. She looked at herself, before she sat down, in the gilt-framed glass and turned back a wisp of her short dark-gold hair. Her face was oval; she posed it to one side; she said, "Of course it has been a disappointment that we had no children. If there had been a son to support Richard on the Board . . . Sometimes I feel, quite frankly, the firm should be called Drover, Drover, Drover Willis, not just Drover Willis.

"Richard was touched a few weeks ago," she said, "he told me so, when he met you one Saturday afternoon while he was waiting for me outside the shop, and he saw you working away on your Saturday afternoon, spending your Saturday afternoon with a

Peckham girl, trying to get to know the types. Richard thinks you are brilliant, you know. A fine brain and a sound moral sense, he told me, quite frankly, and he thinks you're absolutely wasted in the personnel research job. The thing about you—and I saw it long before Richard and I'm not just saying it because you're here—you're so young and energetic, and yet so *steady*. I suppose it's being a Scot.

"Not many young fellows of your age," she said, "—I'm not flattering you—and of your qualifications and ability would be prepared to settle down as you have done in a place like Peckham where the scope for any kind of gaiety is so limited, there's nothing to do and there are no young people for you to meet. I'm speaking quite frankly, as I would to my own son if I had one.

"I feel toward you," she said, "as to a son. I hope—I would always hope—to count you as one of the family although, as you know, there are only Richard and me. I was so interested in your conversation the other night about so many things I didn't quite frankly know existed in this area. The Camberwell Art Gallery I knew of course; but the excavations of the tunnel—I had only read of its progress in the *South London Observer*—I didn't dream there was anything so serious and learned behind it."

She tuned and plumped out the cushion behind her. She looked at her pointed toes. "You must sometimes come to town with us. We go to the theater at least once a week," she said.

She said, "The idea that you should come on the Board with Richard in the autumn is an excellent one. It will almost be like having a Willis in the firm. Your way of speaking is so like Richard's—I mean, not just the accent, but well, quite frankly, I mean, you don't say *much*, but when you say something it's the right thing. Richard needs you and I think I'm right in saying it's an ideal prospect for a young man of your temperament, and it means serious responsibility and an established position within a matter of five or six years. You have this way of approaching life seriously, not just here to-day and gone tomorrow, and it appeals to Richard. Richard is a judge of character. One day the firm might be Drover, Willis & Dougal. Just a moment—''

She went over to the window, smoothing her waist, and glanced through the window as a car drew up in the small curved drive. ''Here's Richard,'' she said. ''He's been looking forward to having a serious chat with you this evening, and getting things settled before we go abroad.''

''Is that you, Jinny?''

''Yes.''

''Have you got any milk on the stove?''

''No.''

''When can I come and see you?''

''I'm getting married next week.''

''No, Jinny.''

''I'm in love with him. He was sweet when I was ill.''

''Just when I'm getting on my feet and drawing two pays for nothing,'' Dougal said, ''you tell me—''

''It wouldn't have worked between us, Dougal. I'm not strong in health.''

''Well, that's that,'' Dougal said.

''Miss Cheeseman's thrilled with her autobiography so far,'' Jinny said. ''You'll do well, Dougal.''

''You've changed. You are using words like 'sweet' and 'thrilled.' ''

''Oh, get away. Miss Cheeseman said she was pleased.''

''She doesn't tell me that.''

"Well, she has some tiny reservations about the Peckham bits, but on the whole—"

"I'm coming over to see you, Jinny."

"No, Dougal, I mean it."

Dougal went into Miss Frierne's kitchen and wept into his large pocket handkerchief.

"Are you feeling all right?" she said.

"No. My girl's getting married to another chap."

She filled the kettle and put it down on the draining board. She opened the back door and shut it again. She took up a duster and dusted a kitchen chair, back and legs.

"You're better off without her," she said.

"I'm not," Dougal said, "but I've got a fatal flaw."

"You're not drinking at nights, Dougal?"

"No more than usual."

She lifted the kettle and put it down again.

"Calm down," Dougal said.

"Well, it upsets me inside to see a man upset."

"Light the gas and put the kettle on it," he said.

She did this, then stood and looked at him. She took off her apron.

"Sit down," Dougal said.

She sat down.

"Stand up," he said, "and fetch me a tot of your gin."

She brought two glasses and the gin bottle. "It's only quarter-past five," she said. "It's early to start on gin. Here's to you, son. You'll soon get over it."

The front-door bell rang. Miss Frierne caused the bottle and glasses to disappear. The bell rang again. She went to answer it.

"Name of Frierne?" said a man's voice.

"Yes, what do you want?"

"Could I have a private word with you?"

Miss Frierne returned to the kitchen followed by a policeman.

[117]

"A man aged about seventy-nine was run over by a bus this morning on the Walworth Road. Sorry, madam, but he had the name Frierne in his pocket written on a bit of paper. He died an hour ago. Any relation you know of, madam?"

"No, I don't know of him. Must be a mistake. You can ask my neighbors if you like. I'm the only one left in the world."

"Very good," said the policeman, making notes. "Did he have any other papers on him?"

"No, nothing. A pauper, poor devil."

The policeman left.

"Well, there wasn't anything I could do if he's dead, was there?" Miss Frierne said to Dougal. She started crying. "Except pay for the funeral. And it's hard enough keeping going and that."

Dougal fetched out the gin again and poured two glasses. Presently he placed a kitchen chair to face the chair on which he sat. He put up his feet on it and said, "Ever seen a corpse?" He lolled his head back, closed his eyes and opened his mouth so that the bottom jaw was sunken and rigid.

"You're callous, that's what you are," Miss Frierne said. Then she screamed with hysterical mirth.

Humphrey sat with Mavis and Arthur Crewe in their sitting-room, touching, every now and then, two marks on his face.

"Well, if by any chance you don't have her, it's your luck," Mavis said. "I say it though she's my own daughter. When I was turned seventeen, eighteen, I was out with the boys every night, dancing and so forth. You wouldn't have caught me doing no evening work just for a bit of money. And there aren't so many boys willing to sit round waiting like you. She'll learn when it's too late."

"It isn't as if she parts with any of her money," Arthur

Crewe said. "You don't get the smell of an oil-rag out of Dixie. The more she's got the meaner she gets."

"What's that got to do with it?" Dixie's mother said. "You don't want anything from her, do you?"

"I never said I did. I was only saying—"

"Dixie has her generous side," Mavis said. "You must hand it to her, she's good to Leslie. She's always slipping him five bob here and five bob there."

"Pity she does it," Arthur said. "The boy's ruined. He's money mad."

"What you know about kids? There's nothing wrong with Leslie. He's no different from the rest. They all like money in their pockets."

"Where's Leslie now, anyway?"

"Gone out."

"Where?"

"How do I know? You ask him."

"He's with Trevor Lomas," Humphrey said. "Up at Costa's."

"There you are, Arthur. There's no harm in Trevor Lomas."

"He's a bit old company for Leslie."

"Grumble, grumble, grumble," Mavis said, and switched on the television.

Leslie came in at eleven. He looked round the sitting-room.

"Hallo, Les," Humphrey said.

Leslie did not speak. He went upstairs.

At half-past eleven Dixie came home. She kicked off her shoes in the sitting-room and flopped onto the sofa. "You been here long?" she said to Humphrey.

"An hour or two."

"Nice to be able to sit down of a summer evening," Dixie said.

"Yes, why don't you try it?"

"Trevor Lomas says there's plenty of overtime at Freeze-eezy if anyone wants it."

[119]

"Well, I don't want it," Humphrey said.

"Obvious."

"Who wants to do overtime all their lives?" Mavis said.

"I was just remarking," Dixie said, "what Trevor Lomas told me."

"Overtime should be avoided except in cases of necessity," Humphrey said, "because eventually it reduces the normal capacity of the worker and in the long run leads to under-production, resulting in further demands for overtime. A vicious circle. Where did you see Trevor Lomas?"

"It *is* a case of necessity," Dixie said, "because we need all the money we can get."

"That's how she goes on," Mavis said. "Why she can't be content to settle down with a man's good wages like other people I don't know. With a bungalow earmarked for October—"

"I want it to be a model bungalow," Dixie said.

"You'll have your model bungalow," Humphrey said.

"She wants a big splash wedding," Mavis said. "Well, Arthur and I will do what we can but *only* what we can."

"That's right," Arthur said.

"Dixie's entitled to the best," Mavis said. "She's got a model dress in view."

"Where did you see Trevor Lomas?" Humphrey said to Dixie.

"Up at Costa's. I went in for a Coke on the way home. Any objections?"

"No, dear, no," Humphrey said.

"Nice of you. Well, I'm going to bed, I'm tired out. You still got your scars."

"They'll go away in time."

"I don't mind. Trevor's got a scar."

"I better keep my eye on Trevor Lomas," Humphrey said.

[120]

"You better keep your eye on your friend Dougal Douglas. Trevor says he's a dick."

"I don't believe it," Mavis said.

"Nor do I," said Arthur.

"No more do I," said Humphrey.

"I know you think he's perfect," Dixie said. "He can do no wrong. But I'm just telling you what Trevor said. So don't say I didn't tell you."

"Trevor's having you on," Humphrey said. "He doesn't like Dougal."

"I like him," Arthur said.

"I like him," Mavis said. "Our Leslie don't like him. Dixie don't like him."

"I like him," Humphrey said. "My sister Elsie doesn't like him."

"Is Mr. Douglas at home?"

"Well, he's up in his room playing the typewriter at the moment," said Miss Frierne, "as you can hear."

"Can I go up?"

"No, I must inquire. Come inside, please. What name?"

"Miss Coverdale."

Miss Frierne left Miss Coverdale in that hall which was lined with wood like a coffin. The sound of the typewriter stopped. Dougal's voice called down from the second landing, "Come up." Miss Frierne frowned in the direction of his voice. "Top floor," she said to Merle.

"I'm miserable. I had to see you," Merle said to Dougal. "What a nice room you've got here!"

"Why are you not at work?" Dougal said.

"I'm too upset to work. Mr. Druce is talking of leaving the country for good. What should I do?"

"What do you want to do?" Dougal said.

"I want to go with him but he won't take me."

"Why not?"

"He knows I don't like him."

[121]

Dougal stretched himself out on the top of his bed.

"Does Mr. Druce mention any date for his departure?"

"No, there's nothing settled. Perhaps it's only a threat. But I think he's frightened of something."

Dougal sat up and placed one hand within the other. He shortened his eyesight and peered at Merle with sublime appreciation. "Dougal," he said, "there is a little place in Soho, would you not come to spend the evening and have a chat? Mrs. Druce is just a bit difficult, she watches—"

"Oh, don't," Merle said. "It brings everything back to me. I can't tell you how I hate the man. I can't bear him to be near me. And now, after all these years, the best years of my life, the swine talks of leaving me."

Dougal lay back with his arms behind his head. "What's he frightened of?" he said.

"You," Merle said. "He's got hold of the idea that you're spying on him."

"In what capacity?"

"Oh, I couldn't say."

"Yes, you could."

"If you're working for the police, Dougal, please tell me. Think of my position. After all, I told you about Mr. Druce in all innocence and if I'm going to be dragged into anything—"

"I'm not working for the police," Dougal said.

"Well, of course, I knew you wouldn't admit it."

"What guilty wee consciences you've all got," Dougal said.

"Don't do anything about Mr. Druce, will you? The Board are just waiting for an excuse, and if they get to know about his deals and all that it will only come back on me. Where will I stand if he emigrates?"

"Who tipped Druce off? Was it Trevor Lomas?"

"No, it was Dixie, the little bitch. She's been going in and out to Mr. Druce a lot behind my back."

"Ah well. Take some shorthand dictation, will you, as you're here?" He got up and fetched her a notebook and a Biro pen.

"Dougal, I'm upset."

"There's nothing like work to calm your emotions. After all, you should be working at this moment. Are you ready? Tell me if I'm going too fast:

" 'Peckham was fun exclamation mark but the day inevitably dawned when I realized that I and my beloved pals at the factory were poles apart full stop The great throbbing heart of London across the river spelled fame comma success comma glamour to me full stop I was always an incurable romantic exclamation mark New para The poignant moment arrived when I bade farewell to my first love full stop Up till now I had had eyes for no others but fate—capital F—had intervened full stop We kissed dot dot dot a shudder went through my frame dot dot dot every fiber of my being spoke of gratitude and grief but the budding genius within me cried out for expression full stop And so we parted forever full stop New para I felt a grim satisfaction as the cab which bore me and my few poor belongings bowled across Vauxhall Bridge and into the great world—capital G capital W—ahead full stop Yes comma Peckham had been fun exclamation mark' Now, leave a space, please, and—"

'What's all this about?" Merle said.

"Don't fuss, you're putting me off."

"God, if Mr. Druce thought I was working in with you, he'd kill me."

"Leave a space," Dougal said, "then a row of dots. That denotes a new section. Now continue. 'Throughout all the years of my success I have never forgotten those early comma joyful comma innocent days in Peckham full stop Only the other day I came across the following paragraph in the paper—' Hand me the paper," Dougal said, "till I find the bit."

[123]

She passed him the newspaper. "Dougal," she said, "I'm going."

"Surely not till you've typed it out for me?" he said. "There isn't much more to take down."

He found the paragraph and said, "Put this bit in quotation marks. Are you ready? 'The excavations on the underground tunnel leading from the police station yard at Peckham are now nearing completion full stop The tunnel comma formerly used by the nuns of the Order of St. Bridget comma stretches roughly six hundred yards from the police station bracket formerly the site of the priory unbracket to Gordon Road and not comma as formerly supposed comma to Nunhead. Archaeologists have reported some interesting finds and human remains all of which will be removed before the tunnel is open to the public quite shortly full stop end quotes.' "

"Is this a police report?" Merle said. "Because if so I don't want to do it, Dougal. Mr. Druce would—"

"Only a few more words," Dougal said. "Ready? New paragraph 'When I read the above tears started to my eyes full stop How well did I recall every detail of that station yard two exclamation marks The police in my day were far from—' "

"I can't go on," Merle said. "This is putting me in a difficult position."

"All right, dear," Dougal said. He sat up and stroked her long neck till she started to cry.

"Type it out," Dougal said, "and forget your troubles. It's a nice typewriter. You'll find the paper on the table."

She sat up to the table and typed from her shorthand notes.

Dougal lay back on his bed. "There is no more beautiful sight," he said, "than to see a fine woman bashing away at a typewriter."

* * *

[124]

"Is Mr. Douglas in?"

"He's up in his room writing out his reports. He's busy."

"Can I go up?"

"I'll see if it's convenient. But he's busy. Come inside, please. What name?"

"Elaine Kent."

"Come up," Dougal called from the second landing.

"You may go up," Miss Frierne said. "Top floor." Miss Frierne stood and watched her climbing out of sight.

"You've been putting too much water in the plant," Elaine said, feeling the soil round the potted ivy. "You should water it once a week only."

"People come here to cry," Dougal said, "which accounts for an excess of moisture in this room."

She took a crumpled brown-paper bag from her shopping basket. They were Dougal's socks which had been washed and darned.

"There's talk going round about you," Elaine said. "Makes me laugh. They say you're in the pay of the cops."

"What's funny about it?"

"Catch the Peckham police boys spending their money on you."

"Oh, I would make an excellent informer. I don't say plain-clothes policeman, exactly, but for gathering information and having no scruples in passing it on you could look farther than me and fare worse."

"There's a gang watching out for you," Elaine said. "So be careful where you go at nights. I shouldn't go out alone much."

"Terrifying, isn't it? I mean, say this is the street and there's Trevor over there. And say here's Collie Gould crossing the road. And young Leslie comes up to me and asks the time and I look at my watch. Then out jumps Trevor with a razor—rip, rip, rip. But Collie whistles loud on his three fingers. Leslie gives me a parting kick where I lie in the gutter and slinks after

Trevor away into the black concealing night. Up comes the copper and finds me. The cop takes one look, turns away and pukes on the pavement. He then with trembling fingers places a whistle to his lips."

"Sit down and stop pushing the good furniture about," she said.

"I've gone and worked myself up with my blether," Dougal said. "I feel that frightened."

"Leslie was waiting for Mr. Willis at five o'clock the day before he went on his holidays. I saw him standing behind Mr. Willis's car. So I hung on just to see. And then Mr. Willis came out. And then Leslie came forward. And then Leslie said something and Mr. Willis said something. So I walked past. I heard Mr. Willis say, 'Have you left school?' and Leslie said, 'What's that to you?' and Mr. Willis said, 'I should want to know a good deal more about you before I took notice of what you say'—or it was something like that, Mr. Willis said. And then Mr. Willis drove away."

"Ah well," Dougal said, "I expect to be leaving here next month. Will you cry when I'm gone?"

"I'd watch it."

"Come on out to the pictures," Dougal said, "for fine evening though it is I am inclined for a bit of darkness." On the way out he picked up a letter postmarked from Grasse. He read it going down the street with Elaine.

Dear Douglas,

We arrived on Saturday night. The weather is perfect and this is quite a pleasant hotel with delightful view. The food is quite good. The people are very pleasant, at least so far! We have had one or two pleasant drives along the coast. Quite frankly, Richard needs a rest. You know yourself how he forces himself and is so conscientious.

Richard is very pleased with the arrangements we came to the other evening. It will be so much better to have someone to support him as there are so many Drovers in the firm now. (I almost think, quite frankly, the firm should be called Drover, Drover, Drover Willis instead of Drover Willis!) I hope you yourself are satisfied with the new arrangements. Richard instructed the accountant before he left about your increase and it will be back-dated from the date of your joining the firm as arranged.

I feel I ought to tell you of an incident which occurred just before we left, although, quite frankly, Richard decided not to mention it to you (in case it put you off!). A young boy in his teens waylaid Richard and told him you were a paid police informer employed apparently to look into the industries of Peckham in case of irregularities. Of course, Richard took no notice, and as I said to Richard, there would hardly be any reason for the police to suspect any criminal activities at Drover Willis's! Quite frankly, I thought I would tell you this to put you on your guard, as I feel I can talk to you, Douglas, as to a son. You have obviously made one or two enemies in the course of your research. That is always the trouble, they are so ungrateful. Before the war these boys used to be glad of a meal and a night's shelter, but now quite frankly . . .

Dougal put away the letter. "I am as melancholy a young man as you might meet on a summer's day," he said to Elaine, "and it feels quite nice."

They came out of the pictures at eight o'clock. Nelly Mahone was outside the pub opposite, declaiming, "The words of the double-tongued are as if they were harmless, but they reach even to the inner part of the bowels. Praise be to the Lord, who distinguishes our cause and delivers us from the unjust and deceitful man."

Dougal and Elaine crossed the road. As they passed, Nelly spat on the pavement.

9

Merle Coverdale said to Trevor Lomas, "I've only been helping him out with a few private things. He's good company and he's different. I don't have much of a life."

"Only a few private things," Trevor said. "Only just helping him out."

"Well, what's wrong with that?"

"Typing out his nark information for him."

"Look," Merle said, "he isn't anything to do with the police. I don't know where that story started, but it isn't true."

"What's this private business you do for him?"

"No business of yours."

"We got to carve up that boy one of these days," Trevor said. "D'you want to get carved alongside of him?"

"Christ, I'm telling you the truth," Merle said. "It's only a story he's writing for someone he calls Cheese that had to do with Peckham in the old days. You don't understand Dougal. He's got no harm in him. He's just different."

"Cheese," Trevor said. "That's what you go there every Tuesday and every Friday night to work on."

"It's not real cheese," Merle said. "Cheese is a person, it isn't the real name."

"You don't say so," Trevor said. "And what's the real name?"

"I don't know, Mr. Lomas, truly."

"You won't go back there," Trevor stated.

"I'll have to explain to him, then. He's just a friend, Mr. Lomas."

"You don't see him again. Understand. We got plans for him."

"Mr. Lomas, you'd better go. Mr. Druce will be along soon. I don't want Mr. Druce to find you here."

"He knows I'm here."

"You never told him of me going to Dougal's, week-nights?"

"He knows," I said.

"It's you's the informer, not Dougal."

"Remember. Any more work you do for him's going to go against you."

Trevor trod down the stairs from her flat with the same deliberate march as when he had arrived, and she watched him from her window taking Denmark Hill as if he owned it.

Mr. Druce arrived twelve minutes later. He took off his hat and hung it on the peg in her hall. He followed her into the sitting-room and opened the door of the sideboard. He took out some whisky and poured himself a measure, squirting soda into it.

Merle took up her knitting.

"Want some?" he said.

"I'll have a glass of red wine. I feel I need something red, to buck me up."

He stooped to get a bottle of wine and, opening a drawer, took out the corkscrew.

"I just had a visitor," she said.

He turned to look at her with the corkscrew pointing from his fist.

"I daresay you know who it was," she said.

"Certainly I do. I sent him."

"My private life's my private life," she said. "I've never interfered with yours. I've never come near Mrs. Druce though many's the time I could have felt like telling her a thing or two."

He handed over her glass of wine. He looked at the label on the bottle. He sat down and took his shoes off. He put on his slippers. He looked at his watch. Merle switched on the television. Neither looked at it. "I've been greatly taken in by that Scotch fellow. He's in the pay of the police *and* of the board of Meadows Meade. He's been watching me for close on three months and putting in his reports."

"No, you're wrong there," Merle said.

"And you've been in with him this last month." He pointed his finger at her throat, nearly touching it.

"You're wrong there. I've only been typing out some stories for him."

"What stories?"

"About Peckham in the old days. It's about some old lady he knows. You've got no damn right to accuse me and send that big tough round here threatening me."

"Trevor Lomas," Mr. Druce said, "is in my pay. You'll do what Trevor suggests. We're going to run that Dougal Douglas, so-called, out of Peckham with something to remember us by."

"I thought you were going to emigrate."

"I am."

"When?"

"When it suits me."

He crossed his legs and attended to the television.

"I don't feel like any supper tonight," she said.

"Well, I do."

She went into the kitchen and made a clatter. She came back crying. "I've had a rotten life of it."

"Not since Dougal Douglas, so-called, joined the firm, from what I hear."

"He's only a friend. You don't understand him."

Mr. Druce breathed in deeply and looked up at the lampshade as if calling it to witness.

"You can have a chop with some potatoes and peas," she said. "I don't want any."

She sat down and took up her knitting, weeping upon it.

He leaned forward and tickled her neck. She drew away. He pinched the skin of her long neck, and she screamed.

"Sh-sh-sh," he said, and stroked her neck.

He went to pour himself some more whisky. He turned and looked at her. "What have you been up to with Dougal Douglas, so-called?" he said.

"Nothing. He's just a friend. A bit of company for me."

The corkscrew lay on the sideboard. He lifted an end, let it drop, lifted it, let it drop.

"I'd better turn the chop," she said and went into the kitchen.

He followed her. "You gave him information about me," he said.

"No, I've told you—"

"And you typed his reports to the Board."

She pushed past him, weeping noisily, to find her handkerchief on the chair.

"What else was between you and him?" he said, raising his voice above the roar of the television.

He came toward her with the corkscrew and stabbed it into her long neck nine times, and killed her. Then he took his hat and went home to his wife.

"Doug dear," said Miss Maria Cheeseman.

"I'm in a state," Dougal said, "so could you ring off?"

"Doug, I just wanted to say. You've re-written my early years so beautifully. Those new Peckham stories

[131]

are absolutely sweet. I'm sure you feel, as I feel, that the extra effort was quite worth it. And now the whole book's perfect, and I'm thrilled."

"Thanks," said Dougal. "I doubt if the new bits were worth all the trouble, but—"

"Doug, come over and see me this afternoon."

"Sorry, Cheese, I'm in a state. I'm packing. I'm leaving here."

"Doug, I've got a little gift for you. Just an appreciation—"

"I'll ring you back," Dougal said. "I've just remembered I've left some milk on the stove."

"You'll let me have your new address, won't you?"

Dougal went into the kitchen. Miss Frierne was seated at the table, but she had slipped down in her chair. She seemed to be asleep. One side of her face was askew. Her eyelid fluttered.

Dougal looked round for the gin bottle to measure the extent of Miss Frierne's collapse. But there was no gin bottle, no bottle at all, no used glass. He took another look at Miss Frierne. Her eyelid fluttered and her lower lip moved on one side of her mouth.

Dougal telephoned to the police to send a doctor. Then he went upstairs and fetched down his luggage comprising his zipper-case, his shiny new brief-case and his typewriter. The doctor arrived presently and went in to Miss Frierne. "A stroke," he said.

"Well, I'll be off," Dougal said.

"Are you a relative?"

"No, a tenant. I'm leaving."

"Right away?"

"Yes," Dougal said. "I was leaving in any case, but I've got a definite flaw where illness is concerned."

"Has she got any relatives?"

"No."

"I'd better ring the ambulance," the doctor said. "She's pretty far gone."

Dougal walked with his luggage up Rye Lane. In the distance he saw a crowd outside the police station yard. He joined it, and pressed through with his bags into the yard.

"Going away?" said one of the policemen.

"I'm leaving the district. I thought, from the crowd, there might be some new find in the tunnel."

The policeman nodded toward the crowd. "We've just arrested a man in connection with the murder."

"Druce," Dougal said.

"That's right."

"Druce is the man," Dougal said.

"He's the chap all right. She might have been left there for days if it hadn't been for the food burning on the gas. The neighbors thought there was a fire and broke in. The tunnel's open now, as you see; the steps are in. Official opening on Wednesday. Lights are being fixed now."

"Pity I won't be here. I should have liked to go along the tunnel."

"Go down if you like. It's only six hundred yards. Brings you out at Gordon Road. One of our men is on guard at that point. He'll know you. Pity not to see it as you've taken so much interest."

"I'll come," Dougal said.

"I can't take you," the policeman said. "But I'll get you a torch. It's just a straight run. All the coins and the old bronze have been taken away, so there's nothing there except some bones we haven't cleared away as yet. But you can say you've been through."

He went to fetch the torch. A young apprentice electrician emerged from the tunnel with two empty teamugs in his hand and went out through the crowd to a café across the road.

The policeman came back with a small torch. "Give this to the constable at the other end. Save you trouble of bringing it back. Well, good-bye. Glad to know you. I've got to go on duty now."

This tunnel had been newly supported in its eight-foot height by wooden props, between which Dougal wound his way. This tunnel—which in a few days' time was to be opened to the public, and in yet a few days more closed down owing to three scandals ensuing from its being frequented by the Secondary Modern Mixed School—was strewn with new gravel, trodden only, so far, by the workmen, and by Dougal as he proceeded with his bags.

About half-way through the tunnel Dougal put his bags down and started to pick up some bones which were piled in a crevice ready to be taken away before the official opening. Then he held the torch between his teeth and juggled with some carefully chosen shin bones which were clotted with earth. He managed six at a time, throwing and catching, never missing, so that the earth fell away from them and scattered.

He picked up his bags and continued through the hot tunnel which smelled of its new disinfectant. He saw a strong lamp ahead and the figure of the electrician on a ladder cutting some wire in the wall.

The electrician turned. "You been quick, Bobby," he said.

Dougal switched out his torch and set down his bags on the gritty floor of the tunnel. He saw the electrician descend from the ladder with his knife and turn the big lamp toward him.

"Trevor Lomas, watch out for the old bones, they're haunted," Dougal said. He chuckled what was once a hip at Trevor's head. Then with his left hand he grabbed the wrist that held the knife. Trevor kicked. Dougal employed that specialty of his with his right hand, clutching Trevor's throat back-handedly with his claw-like grip. Trevor went backward and stumbled over the bags, dropping the knife. Dougal picked it up, grabbed the bags and fled.

Near the end of the tunnel, where the light from the big lamp barely reached, Trevor caught up with him and delivered to Dougal a stab in the eye with a bone. Whereupon Dougal flashed his torch in Trevor's face and leapt at him with his high shoulder raised and elbow sticking out. He applied once more his deformed specialty. Holding Trevor's throat with this right-hand twist, he fetched him a left-hand blow on the corner of the jaw. Trevor sat down. Dougal picked up his bags, pointing his torch to the ground, and emerged from the tunnel at Gordon Road. There he reported to the policeman on duty that the electrician was sitting in a dazed condition among the old nuns' bones, having been overcome by the heat. "I can't stop to assist you," Dougal said, "for, as you see, I have to catch a train. Would you mind returning this torch with my thanks to the police station?"

"You hurt yourself?" the policeman said, looking at Dougal's eye.

"I bumped into something in the dark," Dougal said. "But it's only a bruise. Pity the lights weren't up."

He went into the "Merry Widow" for a drink. Then he took his bags up to Peckham High Street, got into a taxi and was driven across the river, where he entered a chemist's shop and got a dressing put on his wounded eye.

"I'm glad he's cleared off," Dixie said to her mother. "Humphrey's not glad but I'm glad. Now he won't be coming to the wedding. You never know what he might have done. He might have gone mad among the guests showing the bumps on his head. He might have made a speech. He might have jumped and done something rude. I didn't like him. Our Leslie didn't like him. Humphrey liked him. He was bad for Humphrey. Mr. Druce liked him and look what Mr. Druce has come to. Poor Miss Coverdale liked him. Trevor didn't like him. But I'm not worried now. I've got this bad cold, though.''

10

There was Dixie come up to the altar with her wide
flouncy dress and her nose, a little red from her cold,
tilted up toward the minister.

"Wilt thou have this woman to thy wedded wife?"

"No, to be quite frank," Humphrey said, "I won't."

Dougal never read of it in the newspapers. He was
away off to Africa with the intention of selling tape-
recorders to all the witch doctors. "No medicine man,"
Dougal said, "these days can afford to be without a
portable tape-recorder. Without the aid of this modern
device, which may be easily concealed in the under-
growth of the jungle, the old tribal authority will rapidly become undermined by the mounting influence of
modern skepticism."

Much could be told of Dougal's subsequent life. He
returned from Africa and became a novice in a Fran-
ciscan monastery. Before he was asked to leave, the
Prior had endured a nervous breakdown and several
of the monks had broken their vows of obedience in
actuality, and their others vows by desire; Dougal
pleaded his powers as an exorcist in vain. Thereafter,
for economy's sake, he gathered together the scrap
ends of his profligate experience—for he was a frugal
man at heart—and turned them into a lot of cock-eyed
books, and went far in the world. He never married.

The night after Humphrey arrived alone at the honeymoon hotel at Folkestone, Arthur Crewe walked into the bar.

"The girl's heart-broken," he said to Humphrey.

"Better soon than late," Humphrey said. "Tell her I'm coming back."

"She's blaming Dougal Douglas. Is he here with you?"

"Not so's you'd notice it," Humphrey said.

"I haven't come here to blame you. I reckon there must be some reason behind it. But it's hard on the girl, in her wedding dress. My Leslie's been put on probation for robbing a till."

Some said Humphrey came back and married the girl in the end. Some said, no, he married another girl. Others said, it was like this, Dixie died of a broken heart and he never looked at another girl again. Some thought he had returned, and she had slammed the door in his face and called him a dirty swine, which he was. One or two recalled there had been a fight between Humphrey and Trevor Lomas. But at all events everyone remembered how a man had answered "No" at his wedding.

In fact they got married two months later, and although few guests were invited, quite a lot of people came to the church to see if Humphrey would do it again.

Humphrey drove off with Dixie. She said, "I feel as if I've been twenty years married instead of two hours."

He thought this a pity for a girl of eighteen. But it was a sunny day for November, and, as he drove swiftly past the Rye, he saw the children playing there and the women coming home from work with their shopping-bags, the Rye for an instant looking like a cloud of green and gold, the people seeming to ride upon it, as you might say there was another world than this.